A Reel Threat

Gayle Roper

AnniesFiction.com

Books in the Scottish Bakehouse Mysteries series

Library of Congress-in-Publication Data
A Reel Threat / by Gayle Roper
p. cm.
I. Title
                    2019953703

AnniesFiction.com
(800) 282-6643
Scottish Bakehouse Mysteries™
Series Creator: Shari Lohner
Series Editor: Elizabeth Morrissey
Cover Illustrator: Kelley McMorris

10 11 12 13 14 | Printed in China | 9 8 7 6 5 4 3 2 1

1

Molly Ferris stepped into the backyard of Bread on Arrival, the bakery she owned with her best friends, Laura Donovan and Carol MacCallan, and took a deep breath of the late afternoon air. As the gentle breeze ruffled her short, blonde hair, she felt like clicking her heels together. She wasn't in Kansas anymore—or Chicago to be more accurate. The peace and quiet of Loch Mallaig, Michigan, touched something deep inside her. Instead of traffic and sirens, she heard the chitter of a kingfisher hunting for dinner in the lake across Yooper Boulevard, visible through the trees of Dumfries Park.

She smiled down at her Scottish terrier, Angus, who had followed her outside. "Don't you love it, Angus?"

His answer was a yip followed by a quick circuit of the yard with a prolonged stop at a mound of bush honeysuckle. He sniffed appreciatively at its yellow flowers, which were a bright splash of color along the white picket fence.

Molly walked to the edge of the yard and rested her hands on the recently painted pickets, a shiny white in the warm June sun. She smiled as she watched a pair of kayakers leave the public dock across the street, their oars moving in tandem as they dipped left, then right to traverse Loch Mallaig's namesake lake.

The quiet rumble of a car engine entering the parking lot beside Bread on Arrival drew Molly's attention. "She's here, Angus!"

She and Angus hurried forward and arrived at the lot just as Lindy Raymond was climbing from her midsize sedan. The sun caught in her blonde, naturally curly hair, making it gleam like a halo. She was elegant as always in her cropped white pants and sleeveless coral top. Somehow Lindy never seemed to wrinkle, not even after a six-hour drive from Chicago.

Angus ran ahead of Molly, barking a happy greeting. When he reached Lindy, he sat back, his haunches hovering slightly above the ground as his black tail wagged.

Lindy bent and gave him a rub between his bushy eyebrows. "I've missed you, little guy," she cooed.

With a happy woof, Angus circled Lindy. Greeting over, he trotted back to the yard to continue his explorations.

Molly rushed forward and gave her dear friend a warm hug. "I've missed you!"

It was only now that she was up close that Molly noted the circles under Lindy's eyes and the air of fatigue that enveloped her. In all their correspondence, Lindy hadn't mentioned being weary, but she clearly was. *Too many hours at work?* Molly wondered silently. *Trouble with Mike or the kids? Or did she have a bad asthma attack that landed her in the hospital?*

Lindy returned Molly's hug, then stepped back and surveyed the beautiful yellow Victorian that housed both Bread on Arrival and Molly's second-floor apartment. "It's way better in real life than in pictures."

Pride surged through Molly. "It is, isn't it?" In truth, it was way better than anything she had imagined too.

Lindy grabbed her oversize leather purse from the front seat and draped the strap over her shoulder. She popped the trunk of her gold Honda Accord and pulled out a rolling suitcase and a large canvas tote.

"I'm so glad your husband and kids didn't mind you coming to visit," Molly said.

"It was now or never for me and a vacation." Lindy pulled up the handle on her suitcase. "Chic Events is booked all summer, and spring has been one thing after another. I badly need some decompression time, and Mike knew it. He sent me on my way with his blessing."

Good, no marriage trouble. "Well, tell him I said thank you." Molly took the tote from her friend and led the way to the exterior stairs that went up to the second level. Her apartment could also be accessed from inside the bakery, but it was closed for the day. "You must be exhausted from that drive. Come get a drink or a nap. Whatever you need."

"I saw the kids off to school this morning, their last Monday of the school year, and started driving. After six hours sitting, I could use a cold drink, a nap, and a walk around the block, probably in that order." Lindy pulled her case to the stairs, lifted it, and followed Molly up to her apartment. Angus trailed along behind, his nails clicking on the treads as he climbed.

"The bakery is locked up for today, so I'll give you a tour later." Molly opened the exterior door that led into the office, then led Lindy inside. "Let's get you settled and get you a little snack, then you can pick between a nap and a tour of the neighborhood."

She showed Lindy into the den with its queen-size sleeper sofa, cozy armchairs, and carefully chosen decor. She'd had to downsize significantly for her move to Loch Mallaig, and although she still occasionally missed some of the possessions she had shed, she'd kept enough to imbue the apartment with homey comfort.

Lindy swept her gaze over the room. "Your sense of style hasn't deserted you here in the back of beyond."

Molly felt a glow at the compliment. For years, she and Lindy had worked together at Chic Events, a prominent Chicago event planning business, and Molly knew Lindy had a very high standard for what pleased her artistic eye.

"I'm so glad you're here." Molly gave her friend another hug. "Come to the kitchen when you're ready, and I'll have something for you to drink. Coffee? Iced tea?"

"Iced tea, please. It was a hot drive with the sun beaming in the car."

While Lindy settled in, Molly arranged scones from Bread on Arrival on a plate and set it on the kitchen table. She was filling two glasses with iced tea when Lindy entered and sat down.

They ate and chatted as if they'd last parted hours earlier instead of months ago. Lindy proudly updated Molly about her teenage kids, Chase and Marin, while Molly told stories about how she and her college roommates had bought the Victorian house—a former funeral parlor—and converted it into the bakery they'd always dreamed of opening together. With Laura helming the kitchen, Carol decorating cakes and handling the books, and Molly focusing on promoting the business, they'd deftly tackled any challenge that came their way—whether it was related to baking or not. Molly neglected to mention the fact that she and her friends had managed to solve a murder or two in between batches of shortbread.

When her tea glass was empty, Lindy stood. "Never mind the nap. I'm ready for my tour. I need to understand why you're here at the North Pole instead of at Chic Events with me."

"Michigan's Upper Peninsula is hardly the North Pole," Molly said. "Although I suppose it's easier to make that argument in June rather than December."

A few minutes later, they stood at the four-foot-high picket fence that separated the bakery's backyard from Dumfries Park with Loch Mallaig beyond. Angus stood between the women, peering between the pickets.

Lindy squinted at the lake. "Is that a loon out there?"

"It is," Molly confirmed. One of the bakery's part-time helpers, Hamish Bruce, was an avid bird-watcher, and he'd given her a crash course in local ornithology. "Isn't it beautiful?"

As they watched, the black-and-white bird dived. It resurfaced several feet to the left. A little fish wiggled in its mouth, then disappeared down the sleek, black throat.

"The circle of life," Lindy muttered.

Molly clipped a leash on Angus, opened the back gate, and led the way through the trees of Dumfries Park and across Yooper Boulevard to the lake's edge. She gazed out over the vast expanse of water and sighed happily.

Lindy laughed. "I can see you're smitten with the place. I must admit it's beautiful. But how do you sleep in all this silence?"

"You learn."

"And what about winter? It's cold enough in Chicago with the wind whipping off Lake Michigan. What's it going to be like even farther north?"

"I thought about that before I committed to the move," Molly said, patiently withstanding her friend's well-intentioned interrogation. "Remember, Carol, Laura, and I went to college not too far from Loch Mallaig. We knew what we were getting into when we relocated here to open the bakehouse. Plus, I lived in Chicago for decades. Harsh winters aren't new to me."

"Yeah, but there's harsh and then there's *harsh*. Sault Ste. Marie isn't that far away, and it's often the coldest place in the continental United States."

Unaffected, Molly turned her face to the sun. "But right now it's wonderful."

They'd walked only a few yards along the water's edge when Lindy gave a long and weary sigh. Molly glanced at her with concern. It was as if Lindy had suddenly wilted, a flower with her perky head facing the sun one moment, a drooping bloom the next. "Are you okay?"

Lindy managed a wan smile. "The long drive took more out of me than I realized. Do you mind if I lie down for a while? We can finish the tour later."

"By all means," Molly agreed quickly, and they started back to the house. "You nap for as long as you want. Then we'll have dinner and you can decide whether you want to come with me to Leaping Lowlanders or stay at the house and relax."

"What in the world is Leaping Lowlanders?"

"It's the local Scottish dancing group," Molly explained.

"I thought you hated dancing."

Molly shrugged. "It's not really my thing, but it's Guid Nychburris Day on Saturday, and the group needed more dancers for their performance since it's a big draw for the festival. Carol, Laura, and I are being good citizens by participating as background dancers, and we have rehearsal tonight."

"And Guid Nychburris Day is . . .?"

Molly grinned. "Good Neighbor Day. It'll be held here in the park, with lots of food and craft booths, including one hosted by Bread on Arrival."

"So for this performance, you dance what? The Highland fling?"

Molly did a little kick as she raised a hand over her head.

"You're kidding." Lindy raised a skeptical eyebrow. "You're really buying into the Scottish town stuff, aren't you?"

"As Scottish as a Scotsman." Molly closed the back gate behind them. "I'm even learning to play the bagpipes."

Lindy rolled her eyes. "Well that sounds like the easiest thing in the world to pick up."

"I'm not saying I'm good, but it's great fun."

"Where did you get a set of bagpipes?" Lindy asked, incredulity continuing to color her tone.

"I bought them on the Internet."

Lindy laughed. "Talk about the old world colliding with the new."

"The seller even threw in a free instruction book."

"A bargain for sure. Does it help?"

Molly grinned as she followed a bounding Angus up the stairs. "The Piping Yoopers let me fumble my way along."

"The Piping Yoopers? Is that the bagpipe equivalent of Leaping Lowlanders?"

"Essentially. We meet every Sunday."

"I get the piping part of the title, but what's a Yooper?"

"Someone who lives in the Upper Peninsula. The UP. Yooper. Get it?" Molly flashed a grin.

A groan was Lindy's only answer.

A little while later, Molly and Lindy walked the few blocks from Bread on Arrival to the Loch Mallaig Community Center, a large brick building with several multipurpose rooms. A nap and Molly's beef stew had revitalized Lindy, and she declared herself eager to dance—or at least try.

As they passed the parking lot, a petite young woman with delicate features and teal streaks in her shoulder-length black hair waved to get their attention. "Hey Molly!" she called, jogging over from the bike rack.

Molly waved in greeting. "Hi, Bridget." She indicated Lindy. "This is my friend, Lindy. We used to work together in Chicago, and she came to visit for a few days. Lindy, this is Bridget Ross. She's studying forensic science at Superior Bay College and works at the bakehouse in her spare time."

The effervescent coed smiled brightly, her hazel eyes sparkling as she shook hands with Lindy. "Welcome to Loch Mallaig. Don't you love it so far?"

"What's not to love?" Lindy answered. "Are you a Leaping Lowlander too?"

While Bridget nodded, Molly said, "Bridget is one of the best dancers in the group."

"Skye's way better than me," Bridget said graciously.

"And Bridget is the reason Carol, Laura, and I got roped into participating in the Guid Nychburris Day performance," Molly said, then added wryly, "Thanks again for your confidence."

"You know you can't say no to this face." Bridget batted her eyelashes, making Molly laugh. They'd only hired Bridget recently, but she already felt like a daughter to Molly and her partners.

"And I thought you were the persuasive one," Lindy said, raising an eyebrow at Molly.

"I got you to come, didn't I?" Molly checked her watch. "Speaking of which, we'd better get inside."

Once inside the practice space, Bridget went to join a group of principal dancers milling at the front while Molly scanned the crowd for Laura and Carol. She spotted them in the back row and beelined over, Lindy in tow.

"Look who's here," Laura said warmly, hugging Lindy. She and Carol had met Lindy a few times when visiting Molly in Chicago. "How long has it been?"

"A few years, at least," Lindy answered.

"So glad you made it safely," Carol said as she took her turn embracing Lindy.

"I'm glad I made it too." Lindy smirked at Molly. "Just in time to join the fun."

"Will you still be here Saturday to perform with us?" Laura asked.

Lindy cringed. "I'm only here to have some fun tonight. I'll be in the audience on Saturday, where I belong."

"Don't be too quick to judge," Carol cautioned. "You may love it." A levelheaded former math teacher, Carol had surprised Molly with her affinity for Scottish dancing, but the tall grandmother of two had channeled her Scottish ancestors and taken to the activity with natural grace.

"It's a blast." Laura tucked a lock of auburn hair behind her ear. "Almost as gratifying as turning out perfect macarons." Once the head chef at one of New York City's trendiest restaurants, Laura had left the fast pace of the big city behind for the fast pace of the Highland fling.

"I can't wait to try. When in Rome, right? Or in Scottishville, USA, I guess." Lindy grinned at Molly.

Molly chuckled affectionately at her friend's enthusiasm and wondered how much of Lindy's gusto would wane after an hour of jumping in time to the music.

The skirl of recorded bagpipes started blaring over the room's loudspeaker, drowning out the murmur of dancers talking.

Dallis Witherspoon, the leader of The Leaping Lowlanders, clapped his hands for attention as he took his place at the front of the room. "Feet in first position," he called in a loud voice to override the wail of the pipes.

Lindy's eyes went wide. "What's first position?"

"Heels together," Molly explained. "Toes as far apart as possible."

"Ballet arms!" Dallis performed the movements as he called instructions.

Along with everyone else, Molly raised her arms in twin arcs.

"Toes pointed," Dallis said.

Molly curled her foot in her dancing shoe, pointing daintily to the side. Or, at least, as daintily as she could muster.

"Bow to the count of six," Dallis continued.

Molly bent at the waist as she was told. *One, two, three down, four, five, six, up.*

"At least I can do this part," Lindy muttered. "How'd I let you talk me into this?"

Molly laughed. "You don't have to dance. You can just watch—if you don't have the guts."

Lindy stayed with it, and they jumped and bounced in time with the music, Molly feeling every one of her fifty-plus years. The Highland fling, for all its apparent simplicity, was not for sissies. Beside her, a pink-cheeked Lindy kept up impressively well. Granted, Lindy was a good ten years younger, and Molly had never known her not to put her all into any endeavor.

"Take five," Dallis called just as Molly began to doubt she could convince her mightily complaining calves to power one more hop.

Molly, Carol, Laura, and Lindy gathered near the wall, where they'd set their belongings, and Lindy grabbed the bottle of water she'd brought at Molly's insistence. "And you do this for fun?"

Molly wiped the back of her hand over her forehead. "We're here temporarily to help the community. Though I will admit that it's good exercise."

"No one could argue with the exercise bit," Lindy said. "I haven't panted this hard in years."

Molly flicked a hand toward their instructor. "Dallis is a personal trainer by day. It carries over to the class."

"Ah, that explains it." Lindy studied the man, who was listening carefully to a pair of obviously smitten teens. With his auburn hair, green eyes, and athlete's build, thirty-year-old Dallis was the quintessential Scotsman. "He's very good-looking—which explains his fan club."

"Several of the single ladies have their eyes on him," Carol said. "He manages to be friendly without being encouraging, which is quite a feat."

"But still, they try." Laura shrugged, clearly amused.

"They certainly do." Molly indicated the attractive woman who had just rushed to Dallis and started talking, edging the teens out of the way. "Take Janae."

"Janae?" Lindy sounded distracted.

Molly glanced at Lindy and found her friend frowning. "What's wrong?"

Lindy blinked and looked at Molly, her expression vague as if she was trying to figure out something that puzzled her. "That woman talking to the teacher is named Janae?"

"Yes, Janae Harbison," Molly said. "She's a really good dancer. All the local kids take lessons from her."

Shaking her head as if to clear it, Lindy continued to stare. "She looks so familiar, yet she doesn't, you know? Do you ever have that feeling? Sort of like when you see the cashier from your local grocery store at a restaurant. You know you should know her, but you don't out of context."

"Like when you see your incredibly strict and crabby math teacher at the movies wearing Bermuda shorts, with his arm around his girlfriend, and *laughing*. I'm still scarred." Molly chuckled at her high school memory, then furrowed her brow. "But how would you know Janae?"

"I'm not sure." Lindy's frown intensified. "But it's going to drive me crazy."

"Okay, everyone." Dallis clapped his hands. "Janae's going to demonstrate what we want this dance pattern to look like."

Dallis aimed a small remote at a stereo, and once more the skirl of the pipes filled the room. Molly watched Janae, amazed at how something as elementary as a bow could be done so elegantly. Her dancing was both beautiful and precise, every movement fully extended and complete. When Janae finished, applause filled the room.

"Now that's what Scottish dancing is *supposed* to look like." Molly glanced at Lindy and was surprised that the frown hadn't left her face. She was staring at Janae.

Janae, her face wreathed in smiles as she enjoyed the ovation, ran her gaze over the crowd. When she saw Lindy, however, her smile fell away and she turned abruptly, putting her back to the room.

"Did she just recognize you?" Molly asked her friend.

"And I recognize her." Lindy appeared dazed. "But how can it be? She's dead."

2

Molly peered at Lindy with concern. "Who's dead?"

"Janae." Lindy said the name as though grinding it between her teeth. "That's what she's calling herself, right?"

Molly studied Janae's rigid back from across the room. "She's obviously not dead, Lindy."

Lindy bobbed her head slowly, seemingly confused and unsure. "Maybe I'm wrong."

Molly relaxed. "I'm sure she only looks like someone you know. Or knew. It's that grocery clerk thing, like you said."

"Mmm." Lindy's eyes narrowed. "I need to talk to her. Then I'll know for sure."

"She's been in Loch Mallaig for years," Carol said. "She runs the local dance studio."

A beautiful teen with strawberry-blonde hair and sparkling blue eyes rushed up to Janae and started talking animatedly, though her words were lost in the general noise of the room. Molly started to point out that she was Janae's daughter, Skye, but stopped when Lindy made a noise of distress and slapped her hand over her mouth. Her face went unnaturally pale, and she swayed.

Molly reached for her friend. "Lindy!"

"It can't be," Lindy whispered. "Can it?"

As they watched, Janae said something that must have upset Skye, because the girl's face collapsed. She assumed the posture of a puppy being scolded, hunching in on herself. Janae grabbed her by the arm and dragged her from the room. The girl glanced back over her shoulder at Dallis, her expression both confused and apologetic. Molly read Skye's lips as she said, "Sorry. Bye."

"She's leaving." Lindy made a move to follow. "I have to talk to her. Who is she?"

"Janae," Molly repeated, growing more concerned about her friend. "Remember?"

"Not Janae," Lindy said. "The girl. Who is she?"

"That's Janae's daughter, Skye," Molly answered.

"Skye." Lindy took a step toward the door. "She's the one I want to talk to. I *need* to talk to her."

Carol and Laura exchanged confused glances with Molly, who shrugged. She thought about Janae's face when she saw Lindy, thought about the woman's turned back, her sharpness with her daughter, and the speed of their departure. Odds were that Janae wouldn't be happy about any contact with Lindy. Molly put a gentle hand on Lindy's arm. "I'm not sure that's a good idea."

"Of course it is." Lindy appeared ready to chase the girl.

Molly shook her head. "Now might not be the best time." Though she wasn't sure what was going on, Lindy's intensity concerned her. Emotional distress could trigger her asthma, and Lindy suffering a life-threatening attack was the last thing they needed. "Maybe another time. You're going to be here for several days."

Lindy glanced around the room at all the dancers and finally gave a jerky nod. "You're right. It's too public."

Relief washed through Molly, but it was short-lived. She noticed the stricken expression on Lindy's face as she collapsed into a nearby chair.

"Okay," Dallis called. "Let's try it again."

The class fell into place, but Molly stayed with her friend, squatting down beside her. It was obvious that Lindy's dancing was over for the night. Her face was now flushed, her eyes overbright. One hand rested on her heart, and the other held her water bottle. The liquid quivered as she trembled.

Lindy turned an appalled expression on Molly, her hand leaving her heart to clasp Molly's arm. "What if you'd never moved here? What if I hadn't come to visit? What if we'd never worked together and become friends? I'd never have known."

"Lindy, what are—"

Before Molly could ask what her friend was talking about, Lindy threw her arms, water bottle and all, around Molly. "But I do know. Thanks to you, I do." Then, eyes wide, Lindy grabbed her purse. "My phone." She began searching. "Where's my phone? Maybe I can get a picture."

Molly stood. "Come on. I think we'd better leave before we disrupt the rehearsal."

Phone now in hand, Lindy bolted for the door. Molly waved goodbye to Laura and Carol, who both appeared worried and confused, then gathered her own belongings and followed Lindy. She found her friend outside, phone pressed to her ear, her face full of disappointment.

"She's gone, Mike." Mike said something, and Lindy nodded. "Right. Tomorrow's another day. I'll call you later. Love you." She disconnected the call and stuck the phone back in her purse. She turned haunted eyes on Molly. "I missed them."

"I'm sorry," Molly said, though she still had no idea what had her friend so upset.

"Oh no! Is rehearsal over already?" A short, redheaded woman came rushing toward them, her face filled with distress. "How will I survive without a Dallis Witherspoon fix?" She put a hand dramatically to her forehead like an overly emoting actress, paused a moment for effect, then scowled. "That's what comes of district-wide faculty meetings. They're always so long."

"Hi, Bitsy." Molly couldn't help but smile at Bitsy Barkley, Loch Mallaig Elementary School's spirited, sharp-witted principal. She was barely taller than her charges, but she could bring a room full of unruly kindergarteners to heel in seconds with her commanding presence. She was a regular at Bread on Arrival, often buying boxes of pastries to reward her hardworking staff, and Molly was very fond of her. "You haven't missed him. They're still rehearsing."

"Thank goodness." Bitsy flashed a grin. "I can still drool from afar."

From the corner of her eye, Molly saw Lindy slowly sink to the ground. It wasn't a faint—it was as if her legs had gone on strike. Her breathing became ragged. She brought her purse close, searched through it, and pulled out an inhaler, her constant companion. She took a deep breath of the medication.

"Lindy!" Molly knelt beside her, her heart tripping over itself with worry.

"Oh dear." Bitsy crouched down on Lindy's other side. She felt Lindy's forehead, peered into her eyes, and felt her pulse.

"I'm okay." Lindy stuck the inhaler back in her purse. "Really. It all just caught up with me. I mean, can you believe it?"

Believe what? Molly still had no idea what was going on.

Her breathing normalized, Lindy scrambled to her knees and started to push herself to her feet.

"Give it a moment." Bitsy reached a hand to hold Lindy down. "Just to be sure." Somehow, though her voice wasn't raised, it was full of authority. Lindy obeyed without question. Bitsy patted Lindy on her back. "So you're visiting Molly, Lindy? Are you from Chicago like she is? Wasn't our weather gorgeous today?"

Bitsy sounded like she was rambling, but Molly saw her checking first her watch, then Lindy. After a minute, she removed her hand from Lindy's back.

With help from the other women, Lindy climbed to her feet. "Sorry if I upset you. It's just so much to take in. Frankly, thinking about it makes me dizzy."

Although Molly was becoming desperate to know what had upset Lindy so much, she wanted to get her somewhere safe before they delved too deep. Her hand still on her friend's elbow, Molly could feel Lindy shaking in continuing reaction to whatever was going on. Would she be able to walk home in this condition? It had been a lovely walk coming, but now she doubted Lindy was up to the three-block return trip. Fortunately, Bitsy had a solution.

"Tell you what." Bitsy continued to speak directly to Lindy in her pleasant, take-charge voice. "I live right around the corner on Balmoral. Let's go to my house and have a cup of tea. Once you're feeling better, Lindy, I'll drive you both home."

Molly beamed with relief. "Thanks, Bitsy. That sounds wonderful."

Bitsy started walking, and Molly and Lindy followed. Noting that Lindy didn't seem to be having any more trouble breathing, Molly relaxed. The crisis had passed—well, one crisis anyway.

They turned the corner, and Bitsy led them to a charming bungalow painted deep marine-blue with white shutters and a bright red door. Pots of well-tended red geraniums, white lobelia, and vibrant green sweet potato vine flanked the porch steps.

As soon as Bitsy opened the door, a white cat, fluffy as a summer cloud, appeared and wound around her ankles. Bitsy bent and picked her up. "This is Miss Priss."

Molly reached out to pet the cat. "She's beautiful."

When Miss Priss began to purr, a rumbling thunder of noise,

Lindy emerged from her thoughts and laughed. "A big noise for a dainty lady."

In no time, they were seated at the kitchen table while Bitsy put on the kettle and got out cups and saucers. Miss Priss arranged herself in a late-day sunbeam on the shelf of the nearby bay window and promptly went to sleep.

Through the window, Molly glimpsed a patio edged with more pots overflowing with colorful blooms, including daisies, zinnias, ageratum, blue salvia, and petunias. Rich, healthy grass filled the rest of the yard. "You seem to have a knack for gardening, Bitsy."

Bitsy grinned. "I love it. I could do with a longer growing season, but when you live in the UP . . ." She trailed off with a shrug.

"I hear that." A series of planters close to the house caught Molly's eye. "Herbs?"

"Basil, oregano, thyme, mint, and rosemary." Bitsy set a stack of napkins and a basket of tea bags on the table. "I love to cook too, and fresh herbs make all the difference. I keep pots on my windowsill all winter."

While she and Bitsy chatted, Molly watched Lindy out of the corner of her eye. The younger woman seemed unaware of the conversation swirling around her, again lost in her thoughts. Agitation showed in every tense line of her body and in a single jiggling foot.

A piercing whistle sliced the air, and Lindy jumped. She quickly relaxed and smiled as Bitsy poured boiling water from the kettle into a ceramic teapot shaped like a cottage with colorful flowers growing around its base.

Bitsy placed the teapot and a plate of cookies on the table, then finally took a seat. She gestured toward the plate. "They aren't Laura's Empire biscuits, I'm afraid."

Molly smiled and selected chamomile tea. "It's hard to compete."

Lindy selected an Earl Grey tea bag, but paused before ripping it open. "Her name's not Janae Harbison, you know. It's Alana Gladstone."

"Janae's not Janae?" Bitsy appeared fascinated. "Why do you think that?"

Lindy's head snapped up as if she heard a challenge in Bitsy's question. "Because I know her. Knew her. She was my brother's girlfriend."

Molly paused in the middle of squeezing the water from her tea bag. "I didn't know you had a brother."

"I don't. Not anymore." Lindy swallowed as a flash of sorrow crossed her face. "He was murdered."

3

"**W**hat?" Molly immediately reached a hand toward her friend. How had she never known? "I'm so sorry."

Lindy managed a weak smile and grasped Molly's extended hand. "It's okay. Well, it's not, but you know what I mean. It was a long time ago. Nineteen years. About five years before I started at Chic Events and met you. I decided not to mention him at work because it upsets everyone to talk of murder."

Molly had to acknowledge the truth of that statement. "What happened? If you don't mind me asking."

"He was pushed off the roof of an apartment building in Chicago." The words rushed out of Lindy as though she just wanted to say it and get it over with. "So much time has passed that many days I barely even think of Nate. But I don't want to forget him. He was a wonderful guy."

"If he was your brother, I'm sure he was," Molly said.

A grateful smile curved Lindy's lips. She gave Molly's hand a squeeze, then released it and returned to the act of preparing her tea. "It was seeing *her* that brought it all back."

The harshness in Lindy's voice gave Molly goose bumps. While Janae wasn't one of Molly's favorite people, she certainly didn't feel the visceral ill will that Lindy clearly did.

"Alana disappeared at the same time Nate was killed," Lindy said after a fraught pause. "We all thought she had been murdered too, but it was one of those cases where the body wasn't found."

Bitsy leaned forward. "And you think Janae is the missing Alana?"

Lindy raised a steely gaze. "I don't think. I know."

"How?" Molly asked. "You didn't recognize her at first."

Lindy waved that idea away. "She's colored her hair and it's in a different style. And she's almost twenty years older than when I last saw her. Besides, I wasn't expecting to see her. You don't expect to see someone who's dead, you know."

"But maybe it's just someone who looks like your brother's girl used to," Molly suggested, wondering if she was playing a voice of reason or a devil's advocate.

Lindy shook her head. "Skye." She said the name as if it explained all. It didn't.

Bitsy leaned forward, elbows on the table. "What about Skye?"

"I'll show you." Lindy started rummaging through her voluminous purse. She pulled out a booklet of photos and flicked through them. She stopped at one and held it out to Molly. "This is Nate."

A handsome young man with strawberry-blond hair and blue eyes stared back at her. It was a masculine version of Skye, right down to the dimple in the right cheek and the strong brow line.

Lindy angled the photo toward herself and ran her finger tenderly over her brother's face. "He was such a good guy. Much too good for Alana."

"I understand what you mean," Bitsy said. "Janae can be a bit—difficult at times."

Surprised at Bitsy's comment, Molly cocked an eyebrow at her in silent request for an explanation. Bitsy held up a hand and shook her head. It was obvious she regretted the statement and wasn't about to say more. Molly bit her lip to keep her own mouth shut as she remembered her own reasons for being wary of Janae.

One night about a month after Molly had moved to Loch Mallaig, Janae had approached her on a quiet afternoon at the bakehouse. As she ignaled to her daughter to wait, she leaned in. "You have a daughter too, don't you?"

Molly smiled as she always did when she thought of her pride and joy. "Chloe. She's a veterinarian."

"How wonderful."

"It is. I'm so proud of her."

"It must have been hard for her, being raised by a single mother."

"I expect it was at times." Especially the nights Chloe had cried herself to sleep over Kevin's death from an adverse reaction to antibiotics.

"Did she mind? Did she find it embarrassing?" Janae asked.

Molly frowned. "I don't think embarrassing is the right word. Heartbreaking is more appropriate."

"Yes, situations like yours can be heartbreaking for a sensitive child."

Molly let out a puff of laughter. "I don't think of Chloe as particularly sensitive. She's been tough when tough was needed."

"It's probably a good thing she doesn't live here." Janae glanced around the bakery's nearly empty main area. "Small towns can have small minds."

Molly blinked. "I beg your pardon?"

"I'm wondering how Loch Mallaig will look on your situation, single mom and all."

"Oh. With sympathy, I hope." Granted, Molly had been a widow for more than eleven years, and she no longer needed or expected sympathy.

Janae nodded thoughtfully, but it wasn't sympathy in her expression. "The success of your business depends in a large degree on your reputation."

"I think you're right." Reputation and delicious baked goods. Hooray for pastry genius Laura, and Carol the wedding cake queen.

"No one needs to know." Janae leaned in. "I can keep a secret."

"Okay?" Molly had lost the gist of the strange conversation.

"Maybe we can work a trade. Silence about your secret in exchange for—"

"Wait a minute!" Anger boiled as Molly realized what Janae was suggesting. "I'm a *widow*, Janae. A single mom because of tragedy. Even if I were never married, I'd still be proud of Chloe, of us, of our family."

Janae had stared at her for a moment, then shrugged and snapped her fingers at Skye. "Come on, Skye. Let's go."

Ever since, Molly had looked at Janae with a jaundiced eye. Lindy's comments were not changing her mind one bit.

Lindy's face clouded as she continued her tale. "None of us liked her for Nate. Sure, she was pretty and fun, and she knew how to turn on the sparkle. But there was something calculated about her. Something false. 'She's not good enough for you,' we told Nate. 'What do you mean? She's perfect!' was always his answer."

Bitsy held out her hand, and Lindy passed the picture to her. The principal's eyebrows shot up. "Wow. Very definite likeness."

Lindy took the little album back and put it in her purse. When she glanced up, her eyes were stormy. "It was all Alana's fault, the whole horrible mess."

Molly frowned. Was Lindy saying Janae—it was hard to think of her as Alana—had caused Nate's death? How? If everyone had thought her dead too, then no one had believed her to be the killer. But perhaps she was the catalyst?

Bitsy leaned forward and asked the question Molly was afraid to. "Can you tell us why you think it was her fault?"

Lindy took a deep breath. "Nate and Alana had been together for a couple of years. He cared for her more than she did for him. We could all see it, but he couldn't. She liked being his princess more than she liked actually being with him, you know? He was so good to her."

Bitsy reached out and scratched Miss Priss on the head. "Princesses can be wearing."

"And expensive." Lindy absently stirred her tea.

"Did Alana dance like Janae?" Bitsy asked.

"Of course she danced like Janae. She *is* Janae." Apparently Lindy heard the snappishness of her words and held up her hands. "Sorry. Yes, Alana danced. She liked to get work with the touring companies coming through Chicago. She wanted to go to New York City and try her luck. She was always so sure she'd be the one picked from the chorus line on opening night when the real star got sick. She expected to have her name in lights and Broadway at her feet."

"A lot of young women have that dream," Bitsy said.

"And there's nothing wrong with that," Lindy said. "The problem wasn't the dream. It was Alana. When she didn't get a part she wanted, she was impossible to be around. She couldn't stand hearing 'no.' I don't know how she ever thought she'd manage in New York where the competition is so much stronger."

"Then why did she come to a small town so far from Broadway?" Molly mused.

"I've been wondering that myself," Lindy replied. "When I knew her, she was totally narcissistic. Manipulative. She needed to be the star, the sun at the center of the universe with everyone else rotating around her."

Bitsy snorted. "Being a star, a sun, or a princess if you're older than ten is impossible in Loch Mallaig. People are too practical."

"Maybe she's changed?" Molly suggested, though she knew it was unlikely.

"I doubt it," Lindy said. "Leopards and their spots, you know. She would do whatever she needed to get what she wanted. She had no qualms about using people. Nate had a good job—he was a tech wizard—and he was willing to spend a lot of his money on her. She loved it. Because he was so honest and a little bit naive, he didn't see she was playing him, but the rest of us did."

"Love is blind," Bitsy said. "Trite but true."

Lindy grabbed a cookie, but instead of eating it, she crumbled it slowly onto her saucer as she spoke. "They lived together for a while. They had a nice one-bedroom place, but she talked him into a bigger apartment with a second bedroom she could use as her studio. She put up mirrors and a barre. She quit her job so she could practice all day." She made a disgusted noise deep in her throat. "She didn't practice. She spent her time swanning around like some A-list celebrity."

Bitsy frowned. "As far as I can tell, Janae works hard for her money these days."

Lindy issued a derisive grunt. "I ought to let her know that Nate made a small fortune from some computer program he designed. The money's been accumulating for years. When the sum reaches a million, we're going to set up a foundation in his name to encourage girls to study math and science."

"What a nice idea." Bitsy topped off her cup. "As I recall, Skye likes math, much to her mother's disgust. Janae wanted a dancer." She smiled at Lindy. "I always thought her father must have been an engineer."

Lindy smiled back. "He was."

"How long were they married?" Molly asked.

"They were never married." Lindy's eyebrows wrinkled in disgust. "She was never married."

"Interesting," Bitsy said. "She called herself Mrs. Janae Harbison when she moved here. She let us all think she was a young widow."

"Of course she did," Lindy scoffed. "She'd love the sympathy. Anything that made her the center of things. That's why she hung on to Nate. He worshipped her." She shook her head. "Nate was devastated when he found out that she was using drugs, and she fell off her pedestal."

"Drugs? Janae?" Surprise colored Bitsy's response.

Lindy nodded. "Painkillers of any kind—whatever she could get her hands on. She'd had an injury dancing, a really bad ankle sprain and torn ligaments. With a couple of pills, she could dance through the pain."

"And she couldn't let go when the ankle got better?" Bitsy asked, then nibbled on a cookie.

"To get the pills she needed after her doctor refused to order another refill, she developed a strong 'friendship' with a powerful dealer named Rick Capuana. He was into other bad stuff too, but drugs and money laundering were his big things."

Miss Priss stood and stretched on the windowsill. With a graceful leap she landed in Lindy's lap. After a start at the unexpected visitor, Lindy smiled and ran a hand down the cat's back as she began to purr loudly.

"Alana was cunning and clever," Lindy continued. "She was seeing Capuana behind Nate's back for several months. Then, like I said, Nate found out about both him and the pills."

"How?" Molly asked, aghast at this story her friend had struggled with alone for so many years.

"They were driving somewhere, and a kid ran into the street," Lindy said. "Nate hit the brakes, and Alana's purse went flying. Her wallet and a beeper fell out—along with a baggie full of pills."

Bitsy leaned forward. "And that was it for him?"

Lindy grimaced. "I wish, but no. Not at all. He told us he loved her and was going to help her, whatever that meant and however long it took. She chose that corrupt Capuana over Nate. Being with him kept her supplied, and he had more money than Nate. Of course, he also had a reputation for a quick temper and violence, but she chose to overlook that. Nate was devastated when she told him to get lost, but the rest of us were so glad."

Bitsy sat back, her face thoughtful. "I had Skye in school, and I encountered Janae—Alana—often over the years. I never saw signs of drug use. Temper, yes. Self-centeredness, certainly. But drugs? Not at all."

Lindy shrugged. "Maybe she got clean when she was pregnant or when she went into witness protection."

"You think she's here in witness protection rather than just making a fresh start?" Molly asked.

"Seems likely, doesn't it?" Lindy responded. "What do you think?"

"That could be," Molly said. "She's in this little town far from the big city and its criminal element, living under an assumed name. She's set up a whole new life. It'd be hard to do without authorities to help."

"And"—Lindy punctuated her statement with a jab of her index finger into the air—"witness protection was probably the only way to save her neck after she got arrested and agreed to testify against Rick Capuana."

Molly struggled to keep her jaw from dropping at Lindy's increasingly convoluted tale about Janae. *Or is it Alana?* Before any more sordid details came out, however, Miss Priss jumped from Lindy's lap back to the windowsill, where she arranged herself daintily in a ball. Lindy stood, apparently taking the cat's move as a signal to leave.

"Thank you, Bitsy." Lindy gave their hostess a quick hug. She had always had a knack for making lifelong friends in a matter of minutes. "For the tea and for listening." She squeezed Molly's forearm. "You both have no idea how much it means to me to tell the story after all this time."

"Anytime, dear." Bitsy flushed with pleasure, then retrieved her purse and led them outside to her red MINI Cooper convertible.

"Your car matches your front door," Lindy said with a laugh.

Bitsy chuckled. "Or my door matches my car."

Although Lindy's and Bitsy's moods were lightened significantly, Molly couldn't help but fret over the details of her friend's story as Bitsy drove them back to Bread on Arrival. Could it really be true that longtime Loch Mallaig resident Janae Harbison wasn't who she claimed to be?

4

After climbing out of the MINI Cooper in the bakehouse parking lot, Molly and Lindy waved to Bitsy. As the convertible's taillights faded into the distance, Molly started toward the exterior steps leading to her apartment.

"I'm going to take a walk by the lake." Lindy indicated the water visible through the trees of Dumfries Park. "Want to come?"

Molly smiled. "Good idea. Let me get Angus. He'll need the run after a long day of sleeping."

It was well after nine o'clock at night in mid-June in the Upper Peninsula, and the longest day of the year was approaching. The soft light of twilight still lingered.

"We'll go roaming in the gloaming." Lindy spread her arms. "I didn't realize how much I needed this beauty and quiet."

Molly knew that come winter, cross-country skiers would glide along the path where they now walked and the soft night breeze would be a memory. In the peaceful dusk, it was difficult to imagine such a drastic change of season.

Angus pulled on his leash and zigzagged from one side of the path to the other as if fearful he'd miss an interesting smell. Every so often, he'd run back to check in with Molly and Lindy. Then he'd zip ahead again, his tail wagging happily.

As they strolled along the lake path, they encountered other dog walkers, joggers, and bike riders. In typical small-town fashion, everyone waved or called a greeting.

"It's unnatural," Lindy said after their fifth or sixth such interaction. "Take that jogger who just said good evening to us. Do you know him?"

Molly shook her head. "Never saw him before."

"So you spoke to a stranger. Ever heard of stranger danger?"

"I spoke to a neighbor."

"How do you know he's a neighbor?" Lindy's tone was cutting. "Maybe he's one of Rick Capuana's hitmen, here to do Alana in."

Molly nearly laughed, until she realized how upset her friend must be to suggest such a thing. Before she could respond, a man walking a rottweiler approached, and Angus charged right up to the much larger dog to say hello. The rottweiler stared down at Angus for a moment, sneezed, then walked on. Angus seemed to deflate as his would-be friend ignored him.

"You know he left Nate lying in that alley?" Lindy's voice had softened and was now riddled with sorrow. "Just pushed him off the roof and left."

A chill rolled through Molly despite the warm night.

"I never told Mom how long he was there before someone discovered him," Lindy said. "She was devastated enough, especially having lost my father not long before Nate died."

Molly couldn't imagine such callousness. "No one even made an anonymous call?"

"No. Some homeless guy looking for a place to sleep found him." Lindy stared over the lake. "I think it's the leaving him like that that's the hardest to forgive."

Not knowing what to say, Molly settled for wrapping an arm around Lindy's shoulders and squeezing.

Lindy smiled her appreciation. "I can't talk about Nate with most people. It upsets them too much. Thank you for listening."

"I'm happy to listen. That's what friends do. I'm sorry you suffered so much pain."

"At least Rick Capuana is in prison."

"He pushed Nate?"

Lindy nodded. "He denies it, of course, and the cops never proved it. They found scuff marks in the dirt on the roof, so that's how they know there was a struggle, that Nate didn't jump. They couldn't figure out who the other person was, though. But I know it was Rick."

"He's in jail, though. Why?"

"Courtesy of Alana's testimony about his drug crimes and money laundering. When she disappeared, we figured that Rick got to her somehow. None of us thought of witness protection, but it makes sense now."

After they'd walked the length of Dumfries Park, Molly and Lindy retraced their steps, their return journey full of quiet contemplation.

Lindy released a big sigh as they entered the Bread on Arrival yard. "I feel so much better. I sense a good night's sleep coming on."

"Me too." Molly unleashed Angus, then let him show the way upstairs. "Morning comes early in the bakery business."

"That's a big change, isn't it? At Chic Events, most of our parties or special occasions were at night, and it was often quite late before they were over. Or should I say quite early?"

"The early hour's not too bad now because dawn comes early in summer. In December on the other hand . . ."

Once inside, the women parted company, Lindy heading for the den and Molly her bedroom, where she readied herself for bed. When she climbed in, Angus was curled on the second pillow, already sound asleep, and after a long, surprising day, she was ready to join him.

But that was a foolish hope. Every time Molly closed her eyes, Lindy's story filled her mind, playing like a movie with Lindy's sad eyes as the star. After half an hour of trying to sleep, Molly sat up and turned on the bedside lamp. The sight of Angus curled on himself as he slept helped banish the sinister images from her brain and return a sense of reality. She sighed, then put her elbows on her knees and her head in her hands.

God, here's my question: How do people deal with the overwhelming hurt and distress of someone they love being purposely killed? How do they ever forgive?

Although there was no audible answer, Molly felt a calmness settle over her. *Ah, the mystery of faith.* She lay down and waited to see what would happen. The next thing she knew, her alarm declared the start of Tuesday, a new day.

She dressed quickly, fed Angus, and unlocked the doggie door installed in the office, then wrote a quick note for Lindy. *Come downstairs whenever you want and pick out something for breakfast. If you want protein, there are eggs in the fridge.* She slid the folded sheet under Lindy's door, hoping her guest would sleep long and well. She gave Angus a farewell pat on the head, then stole down the stairs.

Molly joined Carol and Laura in the bakehouse kitchen, where wonderful aromas already spiced the air.

"Good morning," Laura said as she slid a tray of scones into the oven with her usual competency. "I didn't expect to see you so early."

"You're supposed to be reducing hours this week since you have a guest, you know," Carol said from her workstation as she brushed a rectangle of dough with melted butter and sprinkled it with cinnamon and brown sugar.

"Lindy is still sleeping, so it doesn't count." Molly pulled a black apron embroidered with the Bread on Arrival logo—a shortbread cookie bearing a Celtic knot—over her head and tied it. She wasn't quite ready to share her friend's revelations from the previous evening, so instead she asked, "Where should I start?"

"We could use another batch of shortbread dough," Laura suggested as she inserted another pan into the oven. "We'll need extra for the festival."

"You got it." Although Laura and Carol were the more expert bakers, Molly was competent enough to handle some basic recipes in addition to her PR and front-of-house duties. She began working on a batch of shortbread, tumbling the butter into the mixer and beating it until fluffy. She slowly added sugar and flour, then a dash of vanilla extract. Lindy's painful story was pushed to the back of her mind as mental preparation for the upcoming Guid Nychburris Day events took precedence.

As if reading her mind, Laura joined her at the mixer with a clipboard in hand. "Anything else you want to add to the list for the festival?" she asked. "I've got regular and chocolate-dipped shortbread, cinnamon and blueberry scones, Empire biscuits, and Abernethy biscuits."

"I don't think much else will fit on the table," Molly said with a laugh. "Although maybe we should do a tray of traditional frosted cookies. Perhaps with a thistle design or a Scottish flag piped on top?"

"The kids will love those," Laura said, nodding enthusiastically, then returned to her workstation to start another project.

"So what happened last night?" Carol asked as she rolled her dough into a tube and cut it into slices that would become delicious sticky buns. "You and Lindy sure took off in a hurry during rehearsal."

Molly hesitated for a moment, then realized that her friends were sure to have insights into Lindy's tragic tale. Hoping Laura and Carol might offer some advice for how best to help Lindy cope with the unexpected turn of events regarding Janae, she told them everything.

"Her brother was killed because of Janae?" Carol shook her head sadly as she set the sliced dough on a bed of brown sugar, melted butter, and pecans. "That's terrible."

"And you think she's in witness protection right here in Loch Mallaig?" Laura's natural skepticism showed.

"It's possible," Molly said. "She testified against Rick Capuana, who sounds like a truly terrible guy. Rather than risk her disappearing at the hands of some of his goons, the government probably thought it best to make her disappear under less fatal circumstances." Molly transferred her dough to a plastic container. It would need to be refrigerated before it could be rolled flat, cut out, and embossed with the bakehouse's logo.

Laura checked on the balls of bread dough rising in the warm, humid proofing box. "So what happens now? Do you think Lindy will try to meet Skye? That could be a real mess if Janae is opposed."

Molly grimaced. "Agreed. I want to help Lindy because she should have a chance to meet her niece, but I don't want her to do anything hasty that could affect her chances of getting to know Skye."

"What happens if this Capuana guy learns Janae is here in Loch Mallaig?" Carol asked. "Do you think he'd still come after her for testifying against him?"

"He's in prison, so I don't think he's a danger," Molly said.

"What happens when a witness protection hideout is discovered?" Carol slid her tray of sticky buns into the oven. "Do they relocate you someplace else?"

Molly froze at the question. What if Janae and Skye moved on before Lindy got a chance to meet her brother's daughter?

5

B y opening time, enticing breads and pastries were stocked in the display cases, fresh coffee and hot water filled the stainless steel commercial carafes, and clean plates and mugs were stacked and ready for serving. Molly couldn't help but smile as she did a final check of the café area on her way to unlock the door. The custom Northwoods-meets-Highlands chairs were grouped tidily around their matching tables, and the sun was shining through the beautiful stained glass design embedded in the front door.

As soon as the sign was flipped to *Open,* two women bustled in and three cars pulled into the parking lot. The morning went quickly, with Molly and Bridget barely getting a moment's rest as they served a seemingly never-ending stream of customers. The only glaring absence was Lindy, who never ventured downstairs from the apartment for breakfast.

During a long-awaited lull, Molly was thinking about checking on her when Dallis Witherspoon entered the bakery and stopped at the register to say hello.

"Good morning." Molly smiled, trying to remember if she'd ever seen Dallis enter Bread on Arrival as a customer. "Are you breaking the Personal Trainers' Code of Conduct by coming in here?"

"I'm trusting you won't report me to the ethics committee." He grinned, then cleared his throat. "I had some time between clients, and I wanted to be sure you were okay."

"I'm fine," Molly said, slightly confused. "Why would you think otherwise?"

"You rushed out in the middle of class last night."

Molly's heart warmed. How nice to have a handsome young man concerned about her. "It was my friend, Lindy, not me. She had a shock. Leaving seemed best so she could recover."

With a nod, Dallis stepped back to assess the display cases. They were a bit sparse after a busy morning, but everyone on staff made a habit of tidying the contents to ensure the cases didn't look unappetizingly picked over.

"Can I get you something?" Molly asked him.

He gave her a wry smile. "It's all very tempting, but I'd better not."

"You are a very disciplined man."

"Years of practice," he said somewhat grimly, then cocked an eyebrow. "How long have you lived here? A few months, right?"

"Yes, although some days I feel like I've lived here forever. In a good way."

Dallis smiled. "I know the feeling. I've been here about seven years, since shortly after I graduated from college. I'm originally from Connecticut."

"I thought you grew up here," Molly said. "Everyone treats you like you've lived here your whole life."

"It's a very welcoming place. And they were happy to find someone to take over Leaping Lowlanders after the last leader moved to Arizona." He returned to the register and rested an elbow on the counter, then leaned forward. "Can I ask your opinion about something?"

"Sure. Anything but politics."

He laughed, his handsome features brightening briefly before settling back into a much more serious expression. "What if I told you I wasn't always this fit?" he asked quietly.

Molly raised her eyebrows. "I'd be impressed at your transformation."

He glanced down at his trim midsection, which was showcased

by his formfitting athletic clothes. "But would knowing that make you distrust me as a personal trainer?"

The question surprised Molly. "Actually, it'd make me believe in you all the more because you got in shape and stayed that way. You'd be an inspiration."

"Not a loser?"

"Absolutely not." Molly's heart ached at the trepidation in Dallis's voice. "I love the stories in the women's magazines about transformations. 'From the Couch to the Winner's Podium' and all that." She grinned at him.

"So if pictures of me as a pudgy kid with braces and acne hit the Internet, you wouldn't care?"

"Certainly not." Though it was obvious Dallis would care. Molly frowned. "Is someone threatening to release such pictures?"

Dallis glanced around, but Bridget was tidying up the café tables and no other customers were close by. "Are you sure you wouldn't care? I don't want to lose my livelihood."

Something about the trainer's intensity told Molly there had to be more behind his distress than only potential revenue loss, upsetting as that possibility was. Sure, pictures of him as an awkward youth might be a bit embarrassing, but for him it seemed much more. Perhaps the answer lay deep in his childhood. "Did you get bullied when you were a kid?"

He narrowed his eyes sharply, then gave a hesitant nod.

"It was bad?" Molly asked, though she knew her question was foolish. Bullying was always bad.

He bobbed his head, closing his eyes briefly. "It was bad. I've tried to forget it, but it still hurts."

Molly studied Dallis, handsome enough to be on the cover of a men's magazine, but who still saw himself in an imperfect past light. She smiled broadly, her brain's PR wheels whirring. "Instead of forgetting it, why don't you let it become a selling point?" she asked. "Perhaps host a speaking engagement? 'Dallis Witherspoon, From Bullied to Buff!'" She said the words as though reading them off a marquee.

He gaped at her in horror.

Molly patted his arm. "Bring your past out in the open, Dallis, and you take away its power. Use it to promote yourself as someone who won the war with your demons. 'I did it for me and I can do it for you!' You'll have more business than you can handle."

Dallis pulled in a deep breath and blew it out slowly as he thought about her suggestion. "You have no idea how scary that sounds."

Molly bet Dallis had been cute even when he was an awkward kid. After all, he still would have had those bright green eyes and that dark auburn hair. But people had done a good job on him, convincing him he was an unredeemable failure. "What got you into fitness?"

"My sister, Holly, dragged me along to her Scottish dancing class when I was a junior in high school," he answered. "At first I thought it was dumb and just for girls, but I ended up having so much fun."

"You clearly stuck with it," Molly said with a grin.

Dallis chuckled lightly. "Clearly. I started eating better and feeling better, and my confidence grew day by day. Holly and I were even on a competitive dance team for a while. My experience training with the team got me into general fitness and led me to majoring in kinesiology and nutrition."

Molly felt a surge of pride for him. "You certainly showed those bullies, didn't you?"

Dallis's face darkened and he didn't reply. The memories of being taunted were obviously still very painful.

Molly tilted her head. "Are you having a booth at Guid Nychburris Day?"

He blinked at the abrupt change of subject. "Sure. I always do. It's a great way to get new clients and promote The Leaping Lowlanders."

"Did you by any chance document your transformation?"

"Not formally, but I'm sure Holly has lots of pictures from when we were competing." He grimaced briefly, apparently remembering that the photos of his former self were what had prompted this entire conversation. "I did keep a journal, though."

"Wonderful." Molly beamed. "You've got a few days before the festival. Make a video showing pictures of you as you were before you started dancing and changed your eating, then share some of you as you are now. It could play in your booth on a loop on a little TV. You could advertise a special night where you'll tell a long version of your story. Rent the community center, maybe, or talk to Grizela Duff about using the library."

Dallis held up a hand to stop her. "Do you do this all the time?"

"I used to be an event planner before I moved here."

"You certainly have a knack for thinking on your feet. But I'm not sure I have it in me to do what you're suggesting."

"I know the idea of putting yourself out there, airing your so-called dirty laundry, is intimidating," Molly said. "But you can make what was one of the hardest things in your life into one of the best because of the help you can give others who struggle with the same kind of demons."

Although Dallis still appeared vaguely dazed by her rapid-fire ideas when he left, a light in his eyes indicated he wasn't opposed to her plan.

Hoping that she could keep her helpfulness streak alive, Molly decided to leave the register in Bridget's capable hands so she could go check on Lindy. She poked her head in the kitchen to tell Laura and Carol her plan, and both women shooed her away as though Molly had already spent too much time in the bakery that day.

Once upstairs, Molly found her friend in the den, paperback in hand. Angus was curled up beside the sofa, apparently too busy keeping Lindy company to greet his human.

"Good book?" Molly asked from the doorway.

"Who knows? I've been wanting to dig into it for almost a year, but I'm reading the same page over and over, and I have no idea what it says." Lindy sighed, then closed the book and glanced up. Molly suppressed a cringe. The dark circles beneath Lindy's eyes had deepened from a sleepless night, and it appeared as if she'd been crying. This vacation, which was supposed to restore her, was having the opposite effect. "All I can think about is Skye."

"Let's go have lunch. You need to get out."

"Probably. It can't be worse than sitting here thinking sad thoughts."

Molly led the way downstairs, leaving an unhappy Angus behind. She and Lindy walked across the street to Neeps and Tatties, a popular local restaurant that served classic Scottish fare.

Lindy studied the sign. "What in the world does that mean?"

"Mashed potatoes with rutabaga or yellow turnip and onion." Molly pulled open the front door. "Very Scottish, and very good with meat pasties."

"Pasties?"

"Little meat pies. Very UP."

"I only drove six hours, and it's a whole different culture," Lindy said, some levity returning to her tone.

"They also have Vernor's Ginger Ale on tap," Molly said. "It was created in Michigan, you know, and it cures all ills. Or so they say."

Over lunch, both women kept the conversation carefully neutral. Molly told more stories about moving to the UP and Lindy told more stories about Chic Events and her kids. Neither mentioned Nate, Janae, or Skye.

The moment they walked out of the pub that changed.

Lindy put a hand on Molly's arm. "Show me Alana's dance studio. I need to see where she's been hiding all this time. And her house. I want to see her house."

"Do you think that's wise?"

"I have no idea. I just know I need to see those places."

Molly took a deep breath and drove to Dancing on Air Studio on the corner of Highland and Loch Ness. It was a little storefront with large, tinted windows that made it hard to see inside. Molly pulled into a parking spot across the street, and Lindy stared, then used her phone to take several pictures.

"I'm sending these to Mike and my mom," Lindy said, tapping away at her phone screen.

The studio door opened and a woman stepped outside. She was dressed in black tights and a black leotard, and her long, white-streaked dark hair was pulled into a tidy knot at the back of her head.

Lindy sat forward. "Who's that? She looks familiar."

"Verna Donnelly. You might recognize her from Leaping Lowlanders. She's Janae's business partner, and I think they share a house."

Lindy squinted at Verna. "She looks older than Janae by several years. I wonder if she knows she's working and living with a snake."

Molly thought it best not to comment.

Verna stood with her back to the door, holding it open for a line of little girls in pink tights, black leotards, and an assortment of sneakers or sandals. They filed out, each carrying a small bag that Molly imagined held their ballet slippers. Their mothers followed, chattering and laughing. Once everyone had exited the building en route to the parking lot, Verna disappeared inside the studio. Soon the lot cleared out and only Molly and Lindy remained.

"Do you think *she's* in there?" Lindy asked, her words barbed.

Molly had no doubt *she* was Janae. "I have no idea."

Lindy fell silent for a few moments. "Skye must be a senior. Where's her school?"

"Loch Mallaig High School is on the edge of town with Bitsy's elementary school and the junior high."

Lindy nodded. "Let's go."

Molly made no protest. She drove the few blocks down Loch Ness Lane to the high school, a single, sprawling building surrounded by a parking lot and athletic fields. They pulled to the side of the road and watched as school buses turned into the driveway.

Lindy stared at the building, her expression full of longing. "She's in there somewhere."

"Or climbing onto one of those buses," Molly said.

Lindy breathed out an extended exhale. "I talked it all over with Mike and my mom last night and again this morning. They can't believe I found Alana. They thought she was dead too. When I told them about Skye, well, you can imagine. Mom cried and kept saying, 'I have another granddaughter, part of my Nate. Oh, I love her already.'" Lindy brushed at the corner of her eye.

Molly hoped Skye was able to see the Raymonds not as strangers who interrupted her life but as family who cared about her deeply. She reached over and squeezed Lindy's hand supportively.

"Of course my kids demanded all the details too," Lindy continued. "Marin thinks it's cool she has a beautiful older cousin who can teach her makeup tricks. Chase is concerned because she'll upset the gender balance in the house. 'Three women against Dad and me. Unfair!' I tried to tell him she might never live in our house, but thirteen-year-old boys are deaf when they have a bone to pick."

Molly tried to imagine how she would feel if she discovered she had a niece, a granddaughter, or a cousin who had been deliberately kept from her for eighteen years. There'd be rejoicing, yearning, resentment, love, fear, uncertainty.

The trouble was that she could also imagine how Janae felt. The woman had literally run for her life while Skye was still growing in her body. She'd built a new life here, and she likely hadn't given a second thought to Nate's family losing a chance to know a part of him. She'd seen it as finding safety for Skye and herself from the dire threat that was Rick Capuana. Chances were she never even considered Lindy and the others who had loved Nate. From Janae's point of view it wasn't selfishness—it was survival.

Life could certainly be complicated.

As school buses drove off in different directions, Lindy leaned back against the car seat and patted her chest. "I want to talk to Skye so much my heart hurts. As if there's a big hand squeezing it."

Molly felt the waves of yearning and frustration streaming from Lindy like water flowing from an overburdened dam. She hoped her friend didn't break from the pressure and emotionally flood everyone involved.

"I want to let her know I'm her aunt." Lindy's eyes were bright with intensity. "No, I *need* to tell her I'm her aunt. She needs to know she has family. I need to tell her there are people who long to welcome her, love her, and care for her. She has two cousins. She has a grandmother. She needs to know we want to include her in our lives."

"What if she sees that as taking her away from her mom?" Molly asked.

Lindy was quiet for a moment. "Then we'll have to convince her that's not what we want. She's eighteen. Old enough to make choices about who she spends time with."

Molly bit her lip and mustered every ounce of diplomacy she could. "How do you think Skye might react to meeting you?"

"I don't know." Lindy fiddled with the buttons down the front of her top. "Mike and my mom say I need to stay away from Skye until we figure out how we should approach her." She sighed. "And they're right. It'd be unfair to come up to her and blurt out who I am. She might be scared by the crazy lady. Besides, who knows what Alana's told her about her father and his family?"

"Waiting sounds wise to me, Lindy."

"Me too, much as I don't like it. I want to rush up to her this very minute and throw my arms around her, but I know I can't. We've waited eighteen years already. What are a few more days?" She squared her jaw. "I told them I'm not leaving here without meeting her at the very least."

"I'm glad you have Mike and your mom to help you navigate this situation," Molly said.

Lindy nodded. "Mike's got an appointment with a family lawyer to find out what our rights are—if we have any. Everyone's rights fade compared to the mom's, especially with the dad dead."

"Skye's eighteen. I think it's her rights and wishes that are important now, not Janae's or yours."

Not seeming to hear, Lindy turned a stricken face toward Molly. "What if we have no rights? What if the courts tell us we can't have anything to do with Skye?" Her voice rose with each question. "What if the marshals move them before we can meet her and she disappears again?"

The last question was one to ponder. Molly grabbed Lindy's hand. "Don't get so worked up. You'll make yourself sick."

"I'm already sick. I've felt nauseated ever since I first saw Alana and sick with a combination of fear and excitement from my first glimpse of Skye. And joy too, you know? A part of Nate lives on."

Molly patted Lindy's hand with what she hoped was encouragement, though she felt dubious at best about how this all might play out. From the little she knew of the relationship between Janae and Nate's family, there seemed no reason Janae would take pity on any of them, even Nate's mother, and expose Skye to people she disliked and who disliked her. She could easily see them all as threats, and she might say and do anything to keep her daughter from even meeting her father's family.

Molly decided to cast diplomacy aside and replace it with straight advice. "You have to be careful what you do and how you do it, Lindy, or Skye will be the one who suffers."

"I know," Lindy said. "I've thought about that. In fact, I've done nothing but think about it. The last thing I'd ever want to do is hurt her." She fixed a beseeching gaze on Molly's face. "Can we drive by their house?"

Molly had been expecting this request. "I know where her business is, but not her house," she said before putting the car in gear. "Can you look up the address and directions for me? Try searching for Verna Donnelly's address. From what I hear, the house is in her name."

Lindy complied, then steered Molly through town for the next several minutes. The drive took them out into the rural countryside surrounding Loch Mallaig, so they rolled down their windows and enjoyed the beautiful early summer day. Eventually, Molly turned onto a long, gravel lane.

"If Janae's house is the only one on this road, we're going to be pretty obvious spies," Molly said, but then one driveway veered off, and then another. Molly was about to relax when they rounded a bend and the narrow road dead-ended at a tiny cul-de-sac and Janae's house, according to the GPS.

Molly was surprised at how big and beautiful the place was. Clad in honey-colored cedar with a huge deck, it sat on the edge of a little glen. Plenty of light caught the front, but the other sides were surrounded by mighty evergreens that would protect it from the winter winds. Beyond it was Loch Mallaig, the blue water barely visible through the pines.

The cul-de-sac was so small that Molly couldn't pull her silver Honda Fit around, so she began a multipoint turn to aim them back the way they came.

While Molly maneuvered the car, Lindy studied the house and said, "It's sort of lonely out here."

"Says the city girl who's used to living on top of her neighbors." Molly checked her rearview camera to be sure she wasn't too close to a red car parked behind her. "There are lots of homes like this one on the lake, most of them built by wealthy summer people."

She'd just changed gears for the next part of her turn when the door of the house flew open and Janae stormed out. The white-hot anger etched into the woman's face made Molly's blood run cold.

6

"Well, now we know she's not at the studio," Lindy muttered, watching the woman approach through narrowed eyes.

Janae marched toward the car, her long, light brown hair fanning out behind her. She wore a soft pink top with her jeans, but there was nothing soft about her expression.

"What are you doing here?" Crystal clear through the open car window, the volume and sharpness of Janae's voice made a pair of hummingbirds at a feeder hanging by the door fly away.

Lindy's breathing had become labored—not dangerously so, but enough to make Molly nervous. When Lindy picked up her purse from its place on the floor and held it close, Molly wondered if she was preparing to grab her inhaler.

"Drive, Molly." Lindy's voice shook. "We need to get out of here. Mike said I shouldn't meet with her because she'll twist things against us. I only wanted to see where she lives, not talk with her, and definitely not get yelled at. Besides, I've got nothing to say to her. Let's go!" She made shooing movements with her hands.

But Janae was standing right beside the driver's side door, so Molly couldn't take off. Instead, she said, "Hello, Janae."

"What are you doing here?" Janae repeated, eyes blazing. She bent and peered at Lindy. "As if I didn't know."

"Wrong turn?" Molly offered feebly.

Janae stared in disbelief. "You think I'm stupid or something?"

Molly swallowed. "Sorry. We just wanted to see where Skye lives."

Janae's eyes narrowed and her hands balled into angry fists. She said nothing for a few seconds, but the venom finally spilled out, her growling voice vibrating with hostility. "Where my daughter lives is none of your business. Get out of here. Now! And don't come back. Ever." She pointed her finger at Lindy. "And stay away from my daughter. I mean it!"

Lindy leaned forward, peering around Molly. "Or wh—"

Molly grabbed her friend's knee and squeezed as hard as she could. A cat fight wouldn't help anything. Lindy yelped in surprise, but she got the message and pressed her lips together so tightly they were edged in white. Lindy began to draw ragged breaths in through her nose. She rummaged through her purse and withdrew her inhaler, then quickly took a puff.

Janae opened her mouth as though about to berate them again, but Molly put up a hand. "We're going," she said, and Janae backed away, eyes still ablaze.

As Molly angled the car toward their escape route, Skye emerged from the woods. The teen's head was turned away as she waved goodbye to another girl who was walking toward a neighboring house.

Lindy, inhaler still in her hand, made a little noise as she stared across the yard at her niece through Molly's window. Today the girl's hair hung loose, well past her shoulders, a beautiful mantle of golden red as she strode through a shaft of sunlight. She wore slim jeans and a T-shirt with a ballerina on the front. A blue backpack hung off one shoulder.

"Isn't she beautiful?" Lindy had her hand over her heart again. Molly nodded, relieved that Lindy's breathing once again sounded normal.

Skye caught sight of her mom striding toward her and all the light went out of the girl's expression. Her features hardened and her shoulders squared as if readying for a fight. Even across the yard, Molly could see the resentment in Skye's posture. Clearly all was not well between mother and daughter, quite apart from Lindy.

Janae pointed to the house and said something. Skye ignored her mother, choosing instead to peer over her shoulder and study Molly's car. Molly smiled at the girl, and Skye smiled back and gave a little wave. Janae jerked as though slapped, and Lindy all but swooned as she too waved.

Janae spun on her heel and stormed toward Molly's car, pointing toward the road. "Get. Out. Of. Here!"

Despite having just told Molly to drive away, Lindy murmured, "Go slowly." She craned her neck so she could still see Skye as the car began to move. "She's so beautiful, so like Nate."

Janae returned her attention to Skye, standing between the girl and the car as if to block her view. Skye immediately stepped to the side to get an unobstructed look at her mom's enemy. She smiled and waved again. Lindy waved back.

Janae grabbed her daughter's arm and began berating her, her voice shrill and furious though the words weren't understandable from the growing distance as Molly drove forward. Molly shot glances at the rearview mirror and saw Skye wrench her arm free, then continue to stare at the car for a few moments of outright rebellion before stomping angrily inside. Janae stood in the yard, hands on her hips, watching her daughter, then whipped around to stare daggers at the Fit.

Molly hit the gas.

Lindy twisted in her seat to glare at Janae through the rear window. When they rounded a bend and the house disappeared from view, she sat forward. "See what a shrew she is?" she asked hotly. "Did you hear her yelling at Skye? And she grabbed her! What did Skye do to deserve that? She waved. That's it." Lindy released a huff of frustration. "I want to climb out of this car, run back there, and hug that poor kid."

Molly didn't say anything. She thought Skye had given as good as she got with her defiance, though she certainly had plenty of sympathy for Skye if that sort of behavior was typical for her mother.

Molly turned from Janae's drive onto the main road and headed back to Bread on Arrival. Lindy had her head down as she worked on her phone. Molly realized she'd taken pictures of both Skye and Janae. She texted rapidly, her thumbs flying, and after a short while she hit send.

Not long after, Lindy's phone dinged with an incoming text. "Mike wants to come up and be with me when I meet Skye," she told Molly after she'd read the text. "He might bring Mom along so she can meet her granddaughter. And the kids."

Molly knit her brows. "I thought you weren't going to push meeting her."

"That was before that scene back there. Skye needs us."

Molly wasn't sure about that, but she didn't press the issue. "When will they arrive?"

"Mike can't get away before the weekend, and the kids have exams this week so they can't cut school." Lindy sighed and stared out the window. "I've got to wait until Saturday to approach her."

Saturday suddenly seemed far, far away.

It was well past midnight and the apartment lights were all out, but Molly was still awake, sitting in the comfy armchair in her bedroom and gazing out the window toward the lake. The moon was almost full, and a silver sheen fell over the yard and the park beyond, so bright it looked like a thin layer of snow covered everything. In the distance, the lake was a pewter platter.

She leaned her head back and shut her eyes. A little snore from Angus, fast asleep on her bed, reminded her that he'd be alert and expecting his morning constitutional at his usual time. Her fatigue would be the least of his concerns.

But Molly's own concerns were what kept her awake. Lindy's story kept swirling in her mind like a treacherous whirlpool. Murder. Drugs. An innocent victim. A corrupt dealer. A duplicitous girlfriend. A secret child. Witness protection. Familial complications.

And heart-wrenching sorrow.

The pain of losing her brother still cut Lindy deeply even after all the years, and seeing Skye had both reopened old wounds and inflicted new ones. When Lindy spoke of her brother, which she had over dinner, it was with a combination of pain and pride. Molly understood that. She'd been a widow for eleven long years, and despite the passage of time, she'd occasionally suffer an unexpected sharp stab at both the thought of what Kevin was missing and the fact that she was experiencing life without him.

There'd been Chloe's graduations from high school, college, and veterinary school, then her move to Milwaukee for her dream job. Some day in the future, Chloe would face the pain of not having a father to walk her down the aisle.

Molly blinked against tears. It had to be the late hour and Lindy's sad story that made her own scars more tender.

Sure, Lindy's love for Nate was different than Molly's love for Kevin, but the aching emptiness was sharp and real for both. *I get it, Lindy. And I'm so sorry.*

The hoot of an owl sounded, but otherwise everything was silent, leaving Molly with only her thrumming thoughts for company. The shadows under the trees in Dumfries Park were pitch black, a fascinating contrast to the silvery, moonlit treetops.

She sat up and squinted through the glass. Was she seeing movement in that inky blackness?

Molly inhaled sharply, stiffening in fright, then forced herself to relax. She shook her head at her foolish imagination. She'd been sitting too long contemplating hard thoughts. She needed to take a deep breath and think reasonably, rationally.

Yes, something was out there, but it was probably wildlife, perhaps a raccoon or an opossum. This was the UP, after all. As she watched, though, the thing in the darkness grew larger. *Okay, maybe it's a moose.* She cringed. *Or a wolf.* As whatever it was got closer, the one large thing broke into four separate beings. Molly nearly laughed. It was only kids running from the park, leaving the forbidding darkness and bursting into the moonlight.

But what were they doing out at this hour of the night? Watching from the second floor, Molly couldn't see their faces or determine their ages, but they were moving as if something was chasing them.

The front runner was a girl. Her ponytail swayed as she raced toward Bread on Arrival. When she reached the gate, she opened it, ran through, and tore across the backyard. She disappeared from Molly's view as she headed toward the front of the house. Hard on her heels came a boy and another girl with long, blonde hair, following the same route. The fourth runner, another boy, ignored the gate and, putting a hand on one of the pickets, jumped the fence.

Or tried to.

The boy twisted and writhed, trying to work himself loose, but to no avail. Somehow he had gotten himself stuck on one of the pickets.

Molly leaped to her feet and rushed toward the door. Her sudden movement woke Angus, who jumped from the bed and ran after her, barking as he went.

"Shush, Angus. You'll wake Lindy." Molly glanced at the closed den door when she passed it on her way to the office.

As she and Angus flew down the outside stairs, the sound of the boy's screaming grew louder. Molly pulled her phone out of her robe pocket in case she needed to dial 911.

"I'm coming! I'm coming!" she called as if her assurances would calm the distraught and potentially injured child.

But when she got closer, the words the boy was yelling began to make sense. He wasn't crying in pain and distress. He was screaming in anger at his friends who had disappeared into the night, leaving him hanging.

"Get back here! Cara! Maggie! Ian! Help me!"

Molly stuck her phone back into her pocket as the boy blistered the air with insults for his long-gone friends. She and Angus approached and found him squirming and twisting, trying to break free.

"Are you hurt?" Now that she could assess the situation, Molly was nearly certain he wasn't, but she had to make sure.

For a moment the boy froze, eyes wide as he stared at her. Then his anger resurged. "What's wrong with you, lady? You think it's okay to just show up out of nowhere and scare a guy to death?"

Molly glanced down at her white nightgown and light-blue seersucker robe. She probably did look a bit ghostly in the moonlight, especially when he hadn't seen her coming.

Having stopped barking, Angus now studied the boy and sniffed at his dangling feet, which didn't quite touch the ground. Molly guessed the kid was about twelve or thirteen. His red sneakers were enormous, indicating he'd be tall someday. His face was starting to lose its little-boy fullness.

"Get me down from here!" He peeked over his shoulder toward the park. "Now!"

Molly thought she detected a flash of fear race across his face.

She glanced toward the park too, but all was quiet. And more than slightly spooky. Best unhook the kid and get back inside.

"How are you stuck?" She walked through the still open gate to assess the boy and the fence from the other side. She had to bite back a smile when she saw the reason for his predicament. He had on a pair of baggy mesh gym shorts. When he'd attempted to vault over the fence, one leg hole had caught on a picket. The top cross board that held the pickets together prevented the shorts from sliding all the way down and kept his feet off the ground.

"What's your name?" Molly asked the boy as she returned to the yard, closing the gate behind her.

The boy stared at her as if he couldn't believe her question. "None of your business. Just get me down!"

"What's going on here?"

Molly startled as Lindy appeared from the darkness on the other side of the fence, still wearing the clothes she'd worn earlier. She must have gone for a late-night walk.

"Who's he?" Lindy nodded at the boy, who shot her a dirty glare in response.

"Good question," Molly answered. "He hasn't told me."

"He doesn't want you telling his parents he's running around after curfew on a school night." Lindy walked toward the gate.

"I don't have a curfew," he muttered.

"Bet you will after tonight," Molly said, irritated by his rude attitude. Since he was dependent on Lindy and her for rescue, he could at least be polite. Instead, he scowled at her.

"What's he doing here?" Lindy asked.

Molly shrugged. "He was running from the park, tried to jump the fence, and here he is." She gestured broadly, like a game-show hostess revealing the grand prize.

"Why's he out in the middle of the night?" Lindy let herself into the yard through the gate, closing it behind her.

"I don't know, but it's a good thing I saw him," Molly said. "Otherwise he'd be dangling here until morning."

"You saw him?" Lindy sounded surprised. "You didn't hear him? I heard him from way off."

"Maybe I'd have heard him, but I was sitting by the window and saw him first." Molly shrugged. "I couldn't sleep."

Lindy sighed. "Me neither."

"Hey!" The boy waved his arms. "I'm still here."

Lindy cocked her head at him. "So you are. Well, I think we should cut off his shorts. That's what the police do when someone's stuck. Snip, snip, and he'll be free."

The boy narrowed his eyes at them. "Don't you dare cut my new shorts."

"Then what do you suggest we do?" Molly asked him.

"Lift me," he growled.

"Lift you?" Molly repeated.

"You know." He raised his arms. "So I can get my shorts unstuck."

Lindy shook her head. "He's too heavy."

"And I can't lift that high," Molly added.

"I'll go get scissors," Lindy offered. "Are they in the kitchen drawer?"

"No!" The kid began squirming again.

"If you want us to lift you, tell me your name," Molly ordered.

The boy stared down at his dangling toes, then finally grumbled, "Robby MacDuff."

Molly smiled at him. "Now was that so hard?"

He glared back.

"Okay, Robby, here's what we're going to do." Molly kept her voice bright, mostly to irritate the kid, who eyed her uncertainly. "I'm going to put my shoulder under your midsection like I'm getting ready to do a firemen's carry, and you're going to lean over my shoulder. Then I'm going to straighten, pressing you up to take the strain off your shorts. My friend is going to slide the fabric off the picket. After that, you'll be free." She hoped.

It worked as Molly envisioned, though straightening her legs under Robby's weight was more of a challenge than she'd expected. But soon enough, the boy stood beside the fence, ready to bolt without a word of thanks.

But Molly caught his arm before he had the chance. "We'll drive you home." No way was she letting him continue to wander the streets.

"It's only a couple of blocks," he protested, tugging slightly against her grip. "I'll be fine."

"We're driving you home." Molly spoke each word slowly and clearly.

He frowned. She wondered if he was this unpleasant all the time, or if it was having to accept help from a pair of moms that made him so grouchy. If Chloe had ever acted that way . . .

Robby tugged again and with slightly more power. Molly tightened her hold. She knew that if he pulled hard, he could get free. And if he did, he'd take off, and there was no way they could stop him. She could almost see his brain clicking away as he came to the same conclusion. She braced herself for whatever he'd do next.

But before the boy could make a move, a scream cut the night, so full of terror and distress that Molly froze where she stood.

When she was able to move again, Molly spun toward Dumfries Park even as her heart thudded and her skin rippled with dismay and disbelief. And fright.

"Help! Somebody help me!" A keening sound full of despair followed the ragged words.

Molly raced through the gate, leaving Robby behind. As she ran, she fumbled in her pocket for her phone. This time she did dial 911. "Someone's calling for help in Dumfries Park," she said in a rush when the dispatcher answered. "I don't know who or what the problem is, but it sounds bad."

She tried to run faster but felt like she was moving in slow motion, her feet heavy and awkward. She'd had nightmares like this, trying to run and being unable to. Her body prickled all over. What would she find? What if she couldn't help?

She was thankful to realize that Lindy ran with her. Facing whatever was ahead was less scary with someone beside her. The closer they got, the inkier the darkness under the trees seemed.

Molly ran into the blackness, and it became less dense as she entered. Here and there, moonlight filtered through breaks in the trees' canopy, and if she was careful, she wouldn't run into anything. She brought up her phone's flashlight app, but the light simply made her surroundings appear weirder. The shadows danced as she ran, becoming darker and eerier. The trees grew larger and leaned in menacingly. The ground came alive with roots anxious to reach out and trip her.

Summoning all her courage, Molly followed the sounds of weeping. She realized she was heading toward the great cluster of large rocks called Crag Mallaig that sat midway through the park. The rocks were many and huge, deposited long ago by a retreating glacier in a formation that resembled a castle—if you had a good imagination. Kids loved to climb there by day and sweethearts liked to meet there at night.

Because of Crag Mallaig, no trees blocked the moonlight. Nearing the rocks, Molly saw a woman standing, hand over her mouth, staring at the ground in front of one large rock.

As she and Lindy drew close, the woman turned her shocked face toward them. Molly recognized Verna Donnelly, Janae's housemate and dance studio partner.

"What's wrong?" Molly called. "Are you all right?"

Verna ran to Molly and clung to her. Molly held her tight, able to feel the woman trembling.

"It's Janae!" Verna's voice was rough with tears. "She's dead!"

7

Lindy moved several feet past Molly to view the spot Verna had been staring at. She took a step back and turned her face away as if she couldn't bear to look at what she was seeing.

"Is it . . .?" Molly couldn't bring herself to finish the question.

"Alana." Lindy's face was blank with disbelief. "It's Alana."

Verna tore away from Molly, wrapping her arms around her middle as if trying to hold herself together. "Someone killed Janae. We need help!"

"Help's coming. I already called." Molly grasped Verna's elbow gently. "Come on, Verna. Let's sit over here until help arrives." She led the dazed woman to a series of seat-high rocks where mothers usually waited while their kids climbed.

Verna followed easily. "Why would anyone hurt Janae?" Tears streamed down her face. "And Skye!"

Molly's blood went icy. "Skye's here?" The thought of that beautiful girl being hurt was too terrible.

"No, no." Verna held out a hand to stop that thought. "She's home, sound asleep in her bed. At least she was when I left the house. I think."

Molly felt a wash of sorrow for Skye. Maybe she wasn't hurt physically, but she'd have her heart broken before the night was over. She remembered Chloe's grief when Kevin died, and she'd still had her mother. Poor Skye would have no one. Molly sat up straight. Unless—

"Did she have any family?" she asked Lindy.

Verna answered, thinking the question was for her. "None. She used to say it was her and Skye against the world." Verna slapped her hand over her mouth to hold in a sob. For the first time, Molly noticed blood on Verna's hands.

Lindy watched the grief-stricken woman, her own expression stoic. "Her mom died not too long after she disappeared. They said cancer, but everyone thought it was a broken heart."

"Her mom didn't know about—" Molly flicked her hand to indicate all the things she wasn't sure she should say in front of Verna.

"I don't know." Lindy appeared thoughtful. "Can you tell your family, or do you just disappear from the earth?"

Verna sat up and stared at Lindy. "You're the one who upset her so much, aren't you?"

Lindy took a deep breath. "Probably."

"She wouldn't say why," Verna said.

Lindy nodded. "I'm not surprised."

But Verna was no longer interested in Lindy. She stared at the place where Janae lay, though the dead woman's form was barely visible in the dark. She emitted a low moan. "How do I tell Skye she's all alone now?"

Molly glanced at Lindy. Skye wasn't all alone. She had an aunt, though she probably didn't know anything about her. She also had an uncle and two cousins back in Chicago. And a grandmother.

Flashlights cut the darkness, and the park burst to life as police and first responders bustled into the clearing. Chief Owen Thomson strode forward flanked by two of his officers, Greer Anderson in uniform and Dalziel Murdoch in jeans and a T-shirt half tucked in—no surprise if he was roused from sleep at this late hour.

Handsome resort owner and Molly's childhood friend Fergus MacGregor, who wore the turnout gear of the Loch Mallaig Volunteer

Fire Company, joined the knot of people. He must have been on call that evening, and seeing him helped Molly feel a little less anxious. He had a calming presence—in addition to dreamy blue eyes and a disarming smile.

The police officers' flashlights scanned the area, and before Molly, Verna, or Lindy could tell them where Janae was, Chief Thomson's beam rested on her body. He gestured to Fergus, who, as a volunteer firefighter, was the certified medical first responder on the scene.

With a nod, Fergus stepped forward and knelt beside Janae. Seconds later, he rose and addressed Chief Thomson. "We need to call Oliver."

He meant funeral director Oliver Fitzgerald, Loch Mallaig's coroner, and Molly lost the slight sense of calm she'd started to feel. She shivered at Oliver's name even though she already knew Janae was dead.

She wasn't the only one affected by the mention of the local coroner. Verna lowered her head to her knees and cried, her bloody hands wrapped around her shins. Lindy, on the other hand, stood steady, her face unreadable.

"Murdoch, pictures," the chief commanded. With a nod, Dalziel began photographing the scene from all angles.

Greer stepped from the official cluster and walked to Molly, Verna, and Lindy. The thirtysomething blonde with an athletic build, whom Molly had gotten to know as a fellow member of The Piping Yoopers, crouched so she was level with Verna and Molly. "I'm so sorry, Verna. I know Janae was your friend."

Verna nodded and let out a shaky breath. "Yeah."

Greer let silence stand for a couple of beats, then asked, "Do you have any idea what happened here?"

Verna rubbed at the tears on her cheeks. "She didn't come home, so I came looking for her." She glanced toward where Janae lay and once again wrapped her arms about herself. "She was fine when she left about ten. Upset, maybe mad, but fine."

Greer raised an eyebrow. "Do you know why she was mad?"

Verna shook her head. "All I know is something upset her this evening. She left The Leaping Lowlanders principal dancers practice all worked up. I mean, she rushed out in the middle of rehearsal, pulling Skye with her. When I got home around nine, she and Skye were having a shouting match."

"About what?" Greer asked the question easily, but Molly couldn't wait to hear the answer.

"Skye was unhappy about Janae forcing her to leave class, and Janae was telling her how stupid she was to have a crush on Dallis Witherspoon. Skye yelled back that she didn't like Dallis that way. She likes Caleb Phelps, who's also one of our regular dancers. Then Janae ripped Caleb apart, making Skye cry and rush to her room and slam the door."

"Are such shouting matches common?" Greer asked.

"Too common for my taste," Verna said, "but they usually blow over. Tonight I thought there was an extra-nasty edge to Janae."

Molly shuddered as an unwelcome idea slithered into her mind. What if Janae had pushed Skye too far? What if Skye had done something terrible in her anger? What if, instead of being asleep at home as Verna thought, the teen had slipped out and followed her mother? What if they had another fight . . . and it turned violent?

"At the time I told myself I was overreacting, but now . . ." Verna's voice cracked. "Now I think I was right. I think she was particularly upset."

"Can you tell me why?" Greer pressed.

Verna shot a quick look at Lindy but said only, "I don't know why."

A flicker of her gaze indicated that Greer caught Verna's glance at Lindy, but she continued questioning Verna. "Do you know who Janae was meeting here?"

"I don't know anything." The words came out on a wail.

Greer rested a comforting hand on Verna's knee. "It's okay, Verna. It's okay. I'm merely trying to understand why Janae was here so late."

Verna took a deep breath and nodded. "When she went out, I asked her where she was going, but she wouldn't tell me."

"Did she go out like that often?" Greer asked.

Verna shrugged. "Sometimes."

"But she told you she was coming here?"

"No. I guessed where she'd be."

"You guessed?"

Verna appeared uncomfortable, her hands clenching and unclenching, her eyes blinking rapidly. "I-I knew she met friends—people—here sometimes."

"At night?"

"Sometimes."

Molly followed the conversation with interest. Janae met people at Crag Mallaig at night?

Greer asked the question Molly was now wondering about, given the rocks' nighttime reputation. "Did Janae have a boyfriend, one she met here in secret?"

Verna seemed surprised by the idea. Her hands stilled and the blinking stopped. "No boyfriend. Janae dates lots of guys. She often goes to nearby towns, even over to Marquette, to meet them. Sometimes she drags me with her, but mostly she likes going alone." Her voice caught. "I guess I should say she *liked* going alone."

"So what happened when you got here?" Greer asked.

"I came to the rocks, and I almost tripped over her b-body." Verna swallowed a strangled cry. "I got down next to her and saw her head was bleeding. I put my hand against the wound, but it was too late. She was already gone. That's when I screamed."

"Do you remember hearing or seeing anything that might lead us to who did this?"

Verna shook her head at Greer's question, then paused. "Actually, I heard footsteps heading in that direction." She pointed away from Bread on Arrival, which meant it wasn't the kids she'd heard.

After a few more dead-end questions for Verna, Greer rose. She shifted her attention to Lindy. "I'm Officer Greer Anderson." She held out her hand. "I don't believe we've met."

"Lindy Raymond. I'm a friend of Molly's."

Greer glanced at Molly, who said, "We used to work together back in Chicago. She's visiting me for a few days."

Greer looked from Lindy to Molly and back again. She gestured toward Lindy. "Clothes." Then Molly. "Nightwear." She raised an eyebrow in question.

"I took a nap this afternoon, and then I couldn't sleep tonight." Lindy shrugged. "Lots of things on my mind."

"How did you come to be here in the park?" Greer asked.

Lindy indicated Verna. "We heard her scream, though we didn't know it was her at the time."

Greer looked across the park to Bread on Arrival. "You heard her from inside the house?"

Molly shook her head. "Lindy and I were at the back fence helping Robby. He was stuck on a picket."

Greer appeared understandably confused, so Molly explained about seeing the running kids and Robby's oversize shorts.

"Are you talking about Robby MacDuff?" Greer asked.

"I know him," Verna said. "He's the kid who's convinced he's a direct descendant of Robert the Bruce, the great Scots king. Or, rather, his mother is. She tells everyone Robby is going to be the MacDuff clan chief."

Molly noted a touch of spite in Verna's words. Apparently she and Robby's mother weren't in agreement. Was the disagreement over the ancestry claim or Robby becoming clan chief? Or both? She made a mental note to ask Hamish what he knew about the MacDuff clan. Hamish also believed himself to be a descendant of Robert the Bruce, though as a former history teacher he was a far more reputable source of genealogical information.

Molly wrapped up her story by saying, "I don't know who the other three kids were, but they all ran from the park. I saw them from my bedroom window. When Robby got stuck, I went to help."

"I heard the commotion and came to help too," Lindy said.

But not from inside the house, Molly thought, not liking the frisson of skepticism that the idea emitted. *From somewhere outside.*

"I have one question." A man's loud voice cut through the night. A moment later, coroner Oliver Fitzgerald emerged from the surrounding darkness, wheeling a gurney topped with a black body bag. "Why do people persist in dying at night? What's wrong with taking your last breath at, say, three o'clock in the afternoon?"

"Most people don't know their last breath is going to be their last breath, Oliver," Chief Thomson said evenly. "Especially when it's murder."

Oliver held up a hand as he brought the gurney to a stop. "Apologies. Cranky when awakened." A blue-and-white striped pajama leg peeked out of one leg of his jeans and his pajama top showed under his official windbreaker, which had *CORONER* stenciled on the back in reflective yellow that matched his trademark neon sneakers. "Where's the victim?"

The chief pointed toward the spot where Janae's body lay. Molly was glad she couldn't see much of what must be a gruesome sight from where she sat beside Verna.

With his industrial-strength flashlight leading the way, Oliver approached the body and began a cursory examination. A short time later, he stood upright and shook his head. "Poor woman. Nasty way to die."

Apparently used to the coroner's glib manner, Chief Thomson merely cocked an eyebrow in question.

"I can't give an official answer until after the autopsy," Oliver said, "but I'd say it was a blow to the head with a blunt object."

Verna released a choked sob, then clapped a hand over her mouth.

"Officer Anderson," Chief Thomson said, "will you please escort Ms. Donnelly home?"

Greer nodded and helped Verna to her feet.

"I don't want to leave her," Verna said in a shaky voice. She stared toward Janae as Dalziel Murdoch unzipped the body bag on the coroner's gurney.

"You can't do anything to help her by staying here, Verna." Chief Thomson's voice was kind. "She belongs to the coroner right now."

Her eyes bright with tears, Verna nodded.

Greer steered Verna toward the path that led to the road. "The best thing you can do is go home and be there for Skye."

Molly watched them walk away, her own eyes moist.

Fergus appeared beside her and laid a hand on her shoulder. "You okay?"

She nodded, glad for his concern. There was nothing like the comfort of an old friend, and she and Fergus had known each other since they were teens.

He removed his hand, and her shoulder felt suddenly cold. "Let me walk you home."

"Thanks." Molly glanced toward Lindy and realized that her friend hadn't yet met Fergus. *What an awkward time for introductions.*

"One question before you go, Mrs. Ferris," Chief Thomson said, breaking into her thoughts. "The kids that ran through your yard—did you say they were running from the park?"

"They were," she said. At the chief's thoughtful nod, she added, "They were glancing back over their shoulders, as if they were running from something." She swallowed. "Or someone."

8

While walking back to the bakehouse with her friends, Molly made introductions, then quickly caught Fergus up on the night's events. As she talked, though, she found herself taking quick peeks at Lindy. Her friend strode purposefully with her eyes straight ahead, her brow furrowed as if deep in thought.

What was she pondering? The irony of Janae—Alana—dying so soon after Lindy had discovered that she was alive? Or maybe the difficulty of approaching Skye now that her mother had been killed? If they'd thought the situation was complex before, they'd had no idea how complicated it would become.

They entered the yard through the gate in the picket fence, and Molly waited while Fergus closed it behind them. Despite Angus barking an energetic greeting, Lindy kept walking, still lost in her own thoughts.

Molly watched her friend with unease. Lindy didn't have anything to do with Janae's death, did she? Just because Lindy disliked the woman didn't mean she'd harm her. The fact that Janae had stood between Lindy and Skye wasn't enough motive for murder . . . was it?

Stop it, Molly! she scolded herself. *Lindy is your friend, not a killer.*

At the base of the exterior staircase, Lindy paused. "I'm waking up Mike with this news," she said over her shoulder, then climbed the steps and disappeared inside.

Instead of following, Molly sat on one of the stairs, too agitated to even consider sleeping. Fergus sat beside her. Angus, not wanting to be left out, climbed into her lap. He might not understand what was going on, but he sensed Molly's apprehension.

Molly hugged him. "It's okay, boy. We're okay." Seeming to accept this, the dog collapsed in her lap for a snuggle.

Fergus laughed and gave Angus a chin scratch, then nudged Molly with his shoulder. "Sorry you got pulled into this."

"Me too," she answered wryly.

He chuckled, then they sat quietly for a little while before Fergus broke the silence. "It was nice to finally meet Lindy. I know you've been excited about her visit."

Molly nearly laughed. "So much for the quiet and recuperation she came here for. I don't think she's getting it."

"Are you worried about her?"

Molly winced. "I don't want to be, but she has a history with Janae that won't look good."

"I was actually asking if you were worried about her health," Fergus said. "But it sounds like you have concerns about her guilt."

"I don't want to, but I can't help but wonder . . ." Molly put a hand to her cheek in distress. "Would suspecting her make me a terrible friend?"

"Not necessarily. Do you suspect her?"

Molly hesitated, then said, "I don't think so."

"That's not a very convincing denial."

She slumped. "I'm a lousy friend."

"I think you're a great friend."

Molly felt her cheeks heat and was glad for the darkness so Fergus couldn't see.

Apparently needing something for his hands to do, Fergus reached out and started petting Angus's head. "Why would Lindy hurt Janae?"

"How much time have you got?"

"Plenty."

Molly told him the story of Nate and Alana and the supposed witness protection assignment that had turned her into Janae Harbison. Fergus listened, interrupting only a couple of times to ask a clarifying question.

When Molly finished, Fergus shook his head in wonder. "So Janae has been hiding out here in Loch Mallaig all these years?"

"Crazy, right?"

Fergus scratched his goatee. "Does Chief Thomson know?"

"I couldn't say, but I doubt marshals tell local law enforcement when they place a witness. I spent some time reading about the witness protection program this afternoon while Lindy napped. Most of the people in it are criminals who agree to testify against another criminal who might have them killed to stop the testimony."

"So Janae was put here because she testified against that Capuana guy, who likely would have killed her?"

"Right. I did some research on him too. I'll spare you details, but let's just say he was not a nice person. He's also the guy Lindy says killed her brother, though there was never any way to prove it."

"They say if you kill once, it's easier to do again," Fergus said. "Maybe the chief should be searching for him."

Molly shook her head. "He's in prison, courtesy of Janae's testimony back when she was Alana Gladstone."

"Maybe he has friends who acted for him?"

"But how would any of them know she was here? We only found out by accident and we've only known for about a day."

Angus stood in Molly's lap and stretched, then jumped down and wandered off to explore the yard.

Molly leaned forward, resting her elbow on her knee and her

chin in her hand. "Everything that happened to Nate is terrible, but it happened almost twenty years ago. That's a long time to hold a grudge."

"I take it you're talking about Lindy, not Capuana?"

She buried her face in her hands. "I'm a terrible friend."

"Has Lindy ever struck you as a vengeful person? In all the years you worked together, did you see her keep score and try to get even if someone made her mad?"

"Not at all. The opposite. She was a peacemaker, an encourager."

"Then tell me why you'd even suspect her," Fergus said.

"She was out wandering by herself, walking around because she couldn't sleep. Or so she told me. She doesn't have an alibi."

Fergus angled himself to level his gaze at Molly. "Do you have an alibi?"

She blinked at the question. "I don't, do I?"

He grinned. "So maybe she was just walking around."

"I know. But she appeared out of the darkness when I was trying to help Robby get free. If nothing else had happened this evening, I wouldn't think anything of it. I'd feel sorry for her because she was already worn out when she got here, and being here isn't doing anything to help her recover."

The door at the top of the stairs opened and Lindy stepped onto the landing. "I didn't do it, you know."

Molly looked up at her friend and nodded. Had Lindy heard them discussing her possible guilt? She desperately hoped not. "I thought you'd be in bed by now."

"I was talking with Mike. He pointed out to me that I had a motive and no alibi, so I wanted to tell you it wasn't me. Now I'm going to try and sleep." With a wave, Lindy disappeared.

Fergus raised an eyebrow at Molly. "Well?"

Molly shook her head. "I'm so tired I can't think clearly anymore. I'm ready for bed too."

Fergus stood and offered a hand to pull her to her feet. "Don't worry. It'll all work out."

"From your lips to God's ears," Molly said wearily.

"Chin up. I'll see you Friday for the setup of your Guid Nychburris Day booth."

Somehow the mention of something from normal life made Molly feel lighter. All wasn't awful. There were events to look forward to, like community festivals and Leaping Lowlander performances. The little girls from Dancing on Air Studio were supposed to dance too. Would they still perform now that one of their instructors was dead?

Molly pulled herself out of the depressing thought with a head shake. "Thanks for talking with me, Fergus." Covering her own yawn, she started up the stairs. When she reached the top, she opened the door, and Angus ran inside. She glanced back and found Fergus watching her.

"Just making sure you get safely inside," he said.

She started to smile at his thoughtfulness, but then reality hit her like a bolt of lightning. Of course he wanted to ensure she was safe. There was a murderer on the loose in Loch Mallaig.

9

The next morning, Bread on Arrival experienced a rush of customers the likes of which it hadn't seen since opening day. Amazing what a murder next door could do for the sale of baked goods.

"Did you really find the body?" asked a woman who bought a cranberry-orange scone along with a little container of clotted cream. Her three friends, each holding her own plated scone and cream, clustered around her, all leaning forward to hear Molly's answer.

From her place behind the cash register, Molly merely smiled and told the women what they each owed. The women, clearly frustrated by the lack of inside information, paid and took seats at a table. They were soon deep in conversation as they heaped the clotted cream on their scones and spooned sugar into their coffee or tea. Judging from the covert glances they shot Molly, she was fairly certain that since she hadn't given them the scoop about Janae, they'd be more than happy to create their own scenario.

But she wasn't at liberty to give them any fodder for their coffee klatch. Just before leaving Crag Mallaig the previous night, Chief Thomson had told her and Lindy under no uncertain terms that they shouldn't discuss the evening's events so as not to "muddy the waters" of an official murder investigation.

So instead of feeding the gossip mill, Molly smiled at her customers and talked about the weather and the coming tourist season. All the while, though, she mused about motive, means, and opportunity.

And Lindy.

Her friend had been out walking well past midnight. She understood Lindy having trouble sleeping. After all, Molly herself had been wide awake when all the trouble started, and she was several degrees removed from the gnarled history between Lindy and Janae. But questions remained. Where had Lindy been? Had she done anything but walk? Was her contempt for Janae motive enough to bash her over the head with a blunt object?

As she ran the credit card of a man who bought a dozen bear claws, she hated herself for suspecting Lindy of anything but having a heavy heart. Lindy was her friend. She'd known her for years. She did not commit violent crimes. Molly determined to turn her back on such disloyal thoughts.

She couldn't turn her back on her job, however. With a mental shake, she refocused on the next woman in line, who was offering cash for a poppy seed bagel and a to-go cup of coffee. Other customers peered into display cases or sat around the sturdy pine café tables, which were almost entirely filled. Laura and Carol were in the kitchen baking up a storm. Bridget and Hamish were both behind the counter filling orders for currant-dotted slices of Montrose cake, Scottish parliament cakes—fragrant ginger biscuits nicknamed parlies—and fruit-and-oat trifles called cranachans. All-American sticky buns were disappearing at a good clip too, and the bagels were almost gone already.

Time blurred from then on, and soon it was midmorning. The front door burst open with a pronounced clang of its bell, and in strode an intimidating woman with curly red hair standing out from her head in all directions. She went directly to the showcases and checked the remaining items, her freckled face puckered as though she'd chewed a lemon.

Hamish stopped at the cash register on his way to the kitchen with a load of used coffee mugs. "That's Robby MacDuff's mother,

Isabella," he murmured, his neatly trimmed white beard twitching at his delight in delivering such news. One story Molly had felt free to tell was the near impalement of Robby, and Hamish had been an appreciative audience. "Did I mention earlier that she claims she's a direct descendant of the original Isabella MacDuff?" he asked. "That's the woman who put the Scottish crown on the head of the rebel king, Robert the Bruce, in 1306."

Molly grinned. "Your history teacher is showing."

"Maybe," Hamish continued in a hushed tone, "but anyone who lives in a Scottish-themed town should know the story of Isabella MacDuff and Robert the Bruce."

"And this Isabella MacDuff is a direct descendant?" Molly was about to express skepticism, but then she remembered Hamish's genealogical ties to Robert the Bruce and decided to go along with it. "She certainly dresses like it," she said quietly, referring to Isabella's plaid skirt, paired with a white blouse adorned at the throat by a gold brooch.

"That tartan she's wearing is the ancient MacDuff hunting tartan," Hamish said.

"They have more than one plaid?"

"They do. Several old patterns and a couple of modern. Clan MacDuff, though currently without a chief, still exists, and as a good MacDuff, she wears one of their tartans every day."

"Every day?"

"Every day."

"But isn't she a married-in MacDuff?"

"She was born a MacDuff and married a MacDuff, or so she says." Hamish's eyes sparkled. "Mr. MacDuff was conveniently deceased when she moved here."

"And people suspect he never existed?"

Hamish shrugged. "No one actually says so."

"Where did she move from? Was she born in Scotland?"

Hamish shook his head. "She's as American as you or I, and I don't think anyone knows where she came from. She's very tight-lipped." He left for the kitchen with his dirty mugs.

Isabella MacDuff brought a loaf of raisin bread and a dozen sugar cookies to the register. Molly smiled at her and wondered if she knew about Robby's late-night adventure. If she did, she didn't mention it as she paid for her purchases.

Hamish stopped at the register again, a pan of assorted Abernethy, Empire, and bannock biscuits in his hands and watched out the window with Molly as Isabella walked to her car. "She's a strange one," he said. "She didn't thank you for helping Robby last night, did she?"

"No," Molly told him, "but I wonder if she even knows her son was running around after midnight."

"Want me to catch her and ask?" Lindy asked, appearing at Molly's side. It was the first time Molly had seen her that day.

Molly shook her head. "Let sleeping dogs lie." She pointed at the tray of biscuits in Hamish's hands. "Want an Abernethy biscuit?" Lindy had already tried the other two varieties the day before. "They're the ones with caraway seeds on the right."

"Sure," Lindy said, then plucked a cookie from the tray and took a bite.

"What do you think?" Molly asked as her friend chewed thoughtfully.

"I haven't decided yet," Lindy answered after she swallowed. "Caraway in a sweet cookie is a taste I'm not used to. Not terrible, but not my favorite. I prefer the bannock biscuits."

Noticing that the register's queue was momentarily empty, Molly felt her energy melt away like dew under the morning sun. She'd gotten less than three hours of sleep last night, and it was catching up with her. She signaled to Hamish to watch the register. "I'm taking a break."

"Here." Hamish set down the tray, placed two bannock biscuits on one of the dessert plates they kept behind the counter, and added two tiny containers of jam. "Fresh from the oven. Laura made more when the morning went crazy."

Lindy accepted the dish and took a deep, appreciative breath, then scrutinized the cookies. "Currants and blueberries? Yum."

"Why don't you grab that table that just opened up?" Molly suggested. "I'll get us some coffee."

Once they were settled, Molly broke open her bannock biscuit and spread it with jam. It tasted wonderful, especially with a sip of coffee to wash it down. She closed her eyes for a moment and felt her head slide to the left as sleep attempted a takeover.

She blinked herself alert and took another sip.

"You must be so tired." Lindy piled jam on her own biscuit. "I'm beat, and I got to sleep several hours longer than you."

"The noise from down here didn't wake you?"

"When I finally surfaced, it was the wonderful smells that called to me, not the noise."

"It does smell good in here." After a few months as a bakery owner, Molly was accustomed to the warm, sweet aroma, but she certainly didn't take its magic for granted.

"So are you going to talk to Mrs. MacDuff about her nighttime adventurer?" Lindy asked.

"I doubt it, unless I hear that he's acting like a hooligan. Parents don't usually appreciate someone telling on their kids, even if it's for the good of the kid."

Mutual silence descended, and as it edged into discomfort, Molly bit her lip. She knew she had to ask Lindy some questions. She took a deep breath only to have Lindy beat her to the punch.

"I know I told you I didn't do it," Lindy said, "but I also know you have no reason to believe me. I've got motive. I could have made an opportunity. I don't know about the means, but I guess any stout stick would have done the job if swung with enough gusto. Motive, means, and opportunity. You're thinking I look like a shoo-in for the role of murderer, aren't you?"

"I wouldn't say shoo-in . . ." Molly tried to smile.

"I get it. I pop up out of nowhere to help with Robby, and you want to know if I came from the park. You're wondering if I had a secret meeting with Alana. You're wondering if I killed her." Lindy reached across the table and clutched Molly's wrist. "I promise you, no secret meeting. No argument either."

"So nothing to worry about," Molly said brightly, feeling better already.

Lindy, however, didn't appear as lighthearted. "Not that I can prove any of it."

"I can't prove where I was before the Robby incident either."

Lindy grinned sardonically. "What a pair we are."

The conversation petered out and they ate their bannock biscuits quietly for a while. Molly felt easier in her mind than she had since they found Verna and Janae.

After taking a sip of coffee, Lindy studied the depths of her cup. "I have to admit I'm not grieving over Alana's death. I know it's awful that anyone would be killed like that, even Alana. Murder is always terrible. It's robbing someone of the chance to be and do all they might have. It's cruel no matter who is killed." She frowned. "But I can't summon any sorrow about her death. I know that makes me an awful person, but that's the way it is."

Molly wasn't sure how to respond. Lindy was right, murder was always bad . . . but Lindy's own brother had also been murdered. Perhaps Lindy had used up all her sorrow on Nate's death.

Lindy ran her finger around the rim of her cup. "She was not a nice person, Molly. She knew how to push people's buttons and how to manipulate them to get what she wanted. I can't imagine her basic personality changed in the years since I last saw her. She'd still be selfish and scheming." She raised her gaze to Molly's, her eyes flinty. "I'm not surprised someone here finally had enough."

Molly realized with a lurch what her friend was implying. She glanced anxiously around the crowded bakehouse, at friendly faces both familiar and unknown. Had one of her Loch Mallaig neighbors murdered Janae?

The door of the bakehouse opened and Greer entered, wearing her Loch Mallaig Police Department uniform. She paused just inside the bakery and took an appreciative sniff as she assessed the room. When she saw Molly and Lindy, she walked over to their table.

"Exactly the people I wanted to see," she said in greeting.

"Good morning." Molly stood and pulled another chair to the table. Was it her imagination, or did Lindy stiffen as Greer approached?

"Can I get you something to eat?" Molly asked the officer. "We've been busy, but Laura and Carol restocked us." She waved toward the display cases as she retook her seat.

Instead of sitting down, Greer studied the array of baked goods. "Everything looks wonderful. How do you decide?"

"You don't. You take more than one," Lindy suggested, any hint of distress gone. She appeared much as she'd been before discovering her brother's ex-girlfriend in Loch Mallaig—weary but relaxed.

Greer laughed. "More than one pastry is the last thing I need, but maybe I'll make an exception." With a grin she wandered to the cases, where she greeted Hamish, who was standing by ready to help her.

As soon as Greer turned her back, Lindy leaned over and grabbed Molly by the wrist. "Don't tell her I was out last night," Lindy hissed.

Molly frowned. "You're one of my best friends, but I can't lie to the police. Besides, they already know you were out."

"They don't know about the wandering. They'll think it sounds suspicious. 'Where did you go?' Nowhere. 'Who did you see?' No one. 'What did you do?' Nothing." She made a huffing sound. "They'll think I went into the park and met Alana. Who knows what else they'll think?"

"Lindy, I can't."

"I'm not asking you to lie. Just don't offer information. Let them assume I ran outside with you to help Robby." She gave Molly's wrist one last pleading squeeze and released her.

Molly dropped her hands to her lap.

Lindy leaned forward, her face intent. "Come on, Molly. Please. I've suffered more than my share of hurt from Alana. All I'm asking is that you protect me from more."

Molly's heart pounded. Even though she understood why Lindy was making her request, it made her uncomfortable. She felt unbalanced, like a tightrope walker caught in an unforeseen cross breeze.

"Telling the cops I was wandering aimlessly will only confuse things." Lindy fixed beseeching eyes on Molly. "It's not like I killed her. I didn't even see her until we found the body."

Still, Molly hesitated. She was unnerved by the idea of lying by omission. "Look at it from Officer Anderson's point of view, Lindy. If you don't tell the police and they find out, you'll look bad. If I haven't told them and they find out, I'll look bad."

Lindy gave a little laugh. "You couldn't look bad if you tried. Besides if you don't tell, who will? No one else knows."

"Don't you think they'll discover you and Janae knew each other in the past anyway?" Molly asked.

"Oh, they'll find that out." Lindy waved dismissively. "I wouldn't try to keep that a secret. That's old history. I just don't want to be seen as a person of interest in the current situation."

Fatigue enveloped Molly. She wanted to put her head down on the table and close her eyes. No more dead bodies. No more difficult requests. Only sleep. Then maybe she'd have the strength to parse the ins and outs of Lindy's request.

She was still arguing with her conscience when Greer returned to the table with a slice of Montrose cake and a cup of plain black coffee. She took a seat and forked off a piece of the cake. She chewed, her eyes closed in delight. "This is so good."

"It's the brandy," Lindy said lightly, as if she hadn't a trouble in the world, as if she hadn't just thrust Molly into a dilemma.

Greer frowned. "What brandy?"

Lindy pointed to the officer's plate. "In the cake. Does that count as drinking on duty?"

Greer chuckled and took another bite. "I don't think so."

Molly watched Lindy with discomfort. She was establishing a friendly rapport with Greer—which would be fine if not for her request that Molly have amnesia about her midnight wanderings.

Greer sipped her coffee, then set her mug down. "So tell me, Lindy, what are you doing here in Loch Mallaig?"

Molly frowned. Greer knew the answer to that question. She'd asked it last night. Was she trying to trip up Lindy?

Lindy smiled as if the repeat question didn't bother her. "I'm visiting Molly. We used to work together in Chicago."

"Really?" Greer acted as if she'd never heard this information before. "What did you do?"

"We were event planners at a business called Chic Events. I still am. I came here to see why Molly deserted me." She grinned at Molly, who made herself offer a strained smile back.

"No other reason for coming here?"

Oh, I see. Now Molly knew where Greer was going.

So did Lindy. She shook her head. "No other reason. I was as surprised as I've ever been when I saw Alana Gladstone at Leaping Lowlanders the other night. For nineteen years I've thought she was dead."

Molly sat back and listened as Lindy and Greer discussed what had happened nineteen years ago. It was obvious Greer had done some research.

"So you have plenty of reason to dislike Janae," Greer concluded.

"Plenty," Lindy agreed. "But reason to dislike her is a far cry from a desire to kill her."

Greer nodded, then asked, "Why were you at the scene last night? I'd have thought you'd be asleep at that hour."

Lindy leaned back in her chair. "I had a hard time falling asleep. Then Robby MacDuff got himself caught on the fence. Molly and I were freeing him when we heard Verna scream. I think we told you that last night."

"You did." Greer shifted her focus to Molly. "Why was the kid running through your yard at that hour of the night?"

Molly shrugged. "I'd like to know that myself. He and his friends ran from the woods as if something had frightened them."

"Did he tell you what they saw that upset them?"

"He didn't even want to tell me his name."

"And his friends' names?"

"Cara, Maggie, and Ian," Molly recited. "Not that he told me. He was just screaming after them when they left him hanging."

"I guess they didn't get the memo about leaving no man behind." Greer took another sip of coffee, her eyes wandering to the display cases now that her Montrose cake was gone. "But it won't be too hard to find them. When we do, one of them is bound to break and tell us what they were doing out at that time of night and what, if anything, they saw. Are those Empire biscuits as good as they look?"

The door to the bakery opened as Greer rose and moved to the display case to get her cookie. Before Molly could turn to see who had come in, Lindy gasped, her eyes wide with shock.

Lindy's face was white as a sheet as she whispered, "How is that possible?"

10

Molly twisted in her seat and saw a bald, muscular man wearing black jeans, a black T-shirt, and mirrored sunglasses. His arms were covered with colorful tattoo sleeves, the work of a real artist. He exuded authority and menace.

Behind him were two very large men, also covered in tattoos that wandered up their necks into their hair. The thought of all those needle pricks in sensitive places made Molly's own skin crawl.

The two larger men scanned the bakery as if looking for trouble, not food. Were they bodyguards for the man in black moving toward the display cases? Their stares hooked on Greer, who gazed calmly back at them before they moved on.

Molly swung back toward Lindy. "Do you know him?"

As she got over her shock, Lindy's pale face turned scarlet and her eyes narrowed with anger. She stood abruptly, her chair toppling behind her.

The noise drew the man's attention, and he inclined his head in recognition. "Well, well, well." He smiled but there was no warmth in it, and the hairs on Molly's arms stood on end. Then he sniffed and went to the display cases, his bodyguards lumbering after him.

Molly righted Lindy's chair. "Sit."

Lindy complied, never taking her eyes off the man. "What's he doing here?" she hissed. "He's supposed to be in prison."

Greer returned to the table, plated Empire biscuit in hand. "Is that who I think it is?" she asked Lindy.

"Who is he?" Molly asked, near exasperation at being out of the loop.

"Rick Capuana." Lindy's voice was full of equal parts disbelief and contempt. "But he's in prison. At least he's supposed to be."

"Not any longer, sweetheart," Capuana called from the display cases. Did he have supersonic hearing? "Time off for good behavior."

Molly doubted he'd ever behaved well.

Hamish, his neat facial hair bristling with distrust, set a bag of pastries on the counter for one of the bodyguards to pick up. "Good day, gentlemen." He indicated the door.

Capuana grinned broadly at the heavy-handed invitation to leave. "Not just yet, Hammy," he said, deliberately misreading Hamish's name tag. "The ladies and I need to talk."

"It's okay, Hamish." Greer rested her hand on her utility belt. "I'm sure this gentleman isn't looking for trouble. He knows his freedom depends on his good behavior."

Hamish glanced at Molly, who nodded slightly. He narrowed his eyes a tiny bit, then disappeared into the kitchen without further comment.

Capuana glided to their table like a great predatory snake sliding along the jungle floor looking for his next meal. "Officer." He inclined his head toward Greer, who was standing on alert. "You may sit because you are correct. I don't want any trouble. I like breathing free air too much to create a problem."

Greer's expression remained steely as she sat down. "I imagine you're already in trouble. You've undoubtedly broken the conditions of your release by crossing state lines to come to Loch Mallaig."

He shrugged. "Maybe I asked permission."

"Maybe you didn't."

"I like you." He winked. "Spunky."

Greer rolled her eyes. "A question, Mr. Capuana."

"You know my name." He appeared pleased.

"Your reputation precedes you," the officer responded drily. "Are you armed?"

"Not at all. Not allowed."

Greer raised an eyebrow pointedly at the two bodyguards.

"They've got permits to carry concealed," Capuana said breezily. "But they won't do anything without the word from me. And I have no plans to give such a word."

Molly felt the thick tension swirling around her, and her skin prickled with nauseating anticipation.

Capuana brought over a chair from a nearby table, the wooden legs dragging noisily on the beautiful pine floor, and sat across from Molly and Lindy. He held out his hands, and one of his bodyguards gave him a cup of coffee. The other bodyguard handed him the bag of pastries, and Capuana withdrew a poppy seed bagel and some cream cheese. A plate and knife appeared on the table in front of him, and he set the bagel on it with reverence.

"I missed these," he said. "The BOP—that's Bureau of Prisons, ladies—doesn't have bagels on their menu, one of many flaws in the system. No cookies either, or whatever those little things are." He pointed to the plate Greer held.

"It's called an Empire biscuit," Molly said with false bravado, suddenly intent on dismantling the moment's tension with trivial facts. "A jam sandwich made with shortbread cookies and decorated with icing. It's Scottish, like our town."

"Scottish, eh? That's why all the funny names." He began slathering cream cheese on the bagel. "We're staying at the Hiegate Hostelry. Fancy name for sort of a dump." He lifted his bagel and sighed in anticipation. "It's the simple things you miss, ladies. The simple things."

Molly watched the man in fascination as he bit into his bagel with relish. He was a drug dealer, a money launderer, and maybe a murderer, and he was enraptured by a breakfast food.

Capuana washed his bite down with coffee, then addressed Lindy. "I hear our mutual friend has come to the end of her road. Such a shame." The twinkle in his eye indicated he thought Janae's death was anything but tragic.

Lindy glared at him with loathing. "What are you doing here?"

He shrugged. "Word travels fast when it's of interest to me, and I like to check things out firsthand."

"What does that mean?"

"It means I came to Scottish Town to see Alana. I am not happy with her." He winced in jest. "Or I should say I *wasn't* happy with her."

Lindy frowned. "Did you always know she was here in Loch Mallaig?"

"You think if I'd known, she'd have still been here?"

Molly shivered at the coldness in his voice. No wonder witness protection had been used for Janae.

Capuana took another bite of his bagel and relaxed. He finished chewing and patted his mouth with his napkin before he spoke again. "The feds are good with their secrets." He indicated Greer. "I bet she didn't even know."

"Then how did you know?" Lindy demanded.

Capuana grinned. "It was you, sweetheart. You spilled the beans."

Lindy jolted. "Me?"

"You called home. Your mother, your husband, your kids. They all talked and their friends talked. You can't keep information quiet these days."

"And when did you hear that information?" Greer asked Capuana.

"Specifically?" He made a big show of thinking. "Yesterday afternoon, about one o'clock."

Greer frowned. "And when did you come to Loch Mallaig?"

"What is it, a six-hour drive?" Capuana glanced at his bodyguards. "What's one plus six?"

So he'd arrived in town the previous evening, Molly realized, hours before Janae was killed.

As he chewed another bite of bagel, Capuana eyed Lindy. "I didn't kill her." He delivered the words coldly. "And I didn't kill him."

"So you say." Lindy's tone indicated she didn't believe him on either count.

Having finished his bagel, Capuana pulled a sticky bun from his pastry bag and eyed it like a cobra might eye a mongoose, all hungry and ready to strike. "I didn't like him, your brother. He was such a good boy, all noble and ready to save Alana from the big bad pills and big bad me." He made those good qualities sound shameful and foolish. "Unlucky for him, she preferred the dark side." His expression was mocking as he took a big bite of the bun. He chewed and swallowed, then said, "As for her, someone beat us to it. Never even got a chance to chat with my old friend Alana."

Lindy scoffed, words apparently failing her as much as they failed Molly at that moment.

Capuana paused with the sticky bun halfway to his mouth. "Of course we only wanted to talk when we met her. We'd never do anything to harm her."

Greer pinned the criminal with a calculating eye. "Because you're good at making sure nothing gets traced back to you, right?"

Capuana shrugged and took another bite.

Molly scooted her chair closer to Lindy's, hoping her friend wouldn't feel alone.

"You are a damaged human being who can't comprehend good, or right, or love." Lindy's voice was quiet but firm.

The man laughed. "None of that garbage made me rich."

"Wasn't it your money that put you in prison?" Greer smiled sweetly at him. "Money laundering and tax evasion, as I recall."

"Yeah, a modern-day Al Capone. All he ever did was forget to pay his taxes too." Capuana peeked in his pastry bag and found it empty. He sighed and folded it neatly. "Good stuff here."

"Thank you," Molly said automatically, then nearly rolled her eyes at herself.

"This is your place?" Capuana asked her. "Really great stuff, especially being in the middle of nowhere, you know? I love good food. First thing when I got out, I got a deep-dish Chicago pizza." Capuana abruptly pointed his finger at Lindy. "I gotta talk to you."

Lindy shook her head. "Leave me alone, Rick. You've got nothing to say I want to hear."

"Ah, but I do. I'll save it for later, though." He glanced at Greer, then back at Lindy. "When you're alone."

He gathered his men and sauntered out, leaving the women to wonder if that was a promise or a threat.

11

Molly glanced at Lindy, wondering how her friend had weathered the conversation. If someone as intimidating as Rick Capuana had talked to Molly like that, she'd be hyperventilating and looking for a place to hide.

Lindy sat with her arms wrapped around her middle, holding herself together much as Verna had done the previous night. She lifted a hand and began rubbing between her eyes.

Molly touched her shoulder. "Are you okay?"

Lindy shook her head. "He scares me. He's a terrible man."

"Agreed." Greer stood. "But I don't think he'll harm you. His position is too precarious."

Lindy glared at the police officer. "You only say that because you don't know him. He'll do anything he thinks he can get away with. Anything. He's already gotten away with one murder—my brother's. Why not another?" She glanced in the direction of Dumfries Park and Crag Mallaig.

"You mean Janae?" Greer asked. "You don't know that."

"He was here last night." Lindy's voice heated. "He certainly had motive. Her testimony sent him to prison for almost twenty years."

"I'm sure Chief Thomson will check out his alibi," Greer replied, unruffled by Lindy's vaguely condescending tone.

"And don't forget his goons." Lindy rubbed her forehead again. "They'll do anything he tells them to."

"I'll remind the chief." With a friendly nod, Greer left.

Molly slumped in her chair, so tired her mind was fuzzy. "I need a nap."

Lindy watched Greer's cruiser pull away from its parking spot. "She's not taking him seriously as a suspect."

"Sure she is," Molly reassured her friend.

"She didn't even ask him specifics about where he was last night. She thinks it was me."

Molly startled at the comment. "What in the world makes you think that?"

"You heard all the questions she asked me."

"She's asking everyone questions," Molly said gently.

Lindy raised a skeptical eyebrow. "She barely asked you any."

"She didn't?" Molly blinked and tried to remember.

Lindy shifted to face Molly. "We have to figure this out. We have to do what the local cops aren't doing."

"Come on, Lindy. Give them a chance."

"If you won't help me, I'll do it myself."

Molly took a deep breath. "Do what exactly?"

"Investigate."

"What do you know about investigating a crime?"

"Not much," Lindy admitted. "But I have to be sure my name is clear, not only for me but for Skye. We're probably her only family now. If there's a shadow over my name, why should she trust us?" Tears collected at the edges of her eyes, threatening to drop. "Help me, Molly. Please."

How could Molly say no to her friend? "Okay," she said with a sigh. "But after I take a nap. I need to be able to think clearly."

Lindy nodded vigorously and stood. "Right. We can start by talking to Robby and his friends. We'll ask Bitsy for help finding them, then grill them about what they saw."

"Grill them?"

Lindy flushed. "That's what they say on TV."

"They're teenagers," Molly said as she gathered the plates and mugs on the table. "They are not going to respond to two ladies 'grilling them.'"

"We have to try." Lindy's voice sounded hollow. The stress was clearly getting to her.

"All right," Molly agreed reluctantly. "We'll try." She led the way toward the kitchen, where she deposited their used dishes in the sink.

Glancing up from the pastry dough she was laminating with butter, Laura took one look at Molly and pulled a face. "You need some rest."

"Is it that obvious?" Molly asked, though she knew it was.

"Yep," Laura said, with unabashed honesty. "Go sleep, both of you. We're fine here."

Molly gave a drowsy smile. "You guys are the greatest."

Glancing up from a birthday cake she was frosting, Carol pointed a buttercream-covered spatula at Molly. "We have ulterior motives. You'll be no use to us for Guid Nychburris Day if you're a zombie."

Suppressing a groan at yet another responsibility she didn't currently have the energy to tackle, Molly trudged up the stairs and straight to her bed.

It was early evening when Molly and Lindy arrived at Bitsy Barkley's pretty blue house. Molly, revived by her long nap, rang the bell.

"I'm out back," Bitsy called. "Come on around."

Molly and Lindy circled the house on a flagstone path to the backyard, where Bitsy was kneeling on a foam pad beside one of her planters, this one a large blue enamelware pot brimming with pink geraniums, purple million bells, and blue lobelia.

"What a nice surprise." Bitsy grinned and indicated the comfy chairs on her deck. "Have a seat." While the other women were seating themselves, Bitsy rose and carried a pair of small plastic pots to a recycling bin hidden behind a fence at the edge of the deck, then pulled off a pair of well-used gardening gloves. "I'm adding a little sweet alyssum for some white to bring out the other colors." She laid the gloves on the edge of the deck. "I was about to get myself a glass of iced tea. Can I interest you in some?"

"If it's no trouble." Molly leaned back and enjoyed the colors and fragrances that came courtesy of Bitsy's talented green thumb.

"Can I help at all?" Lindy asked.

"Just relax," the principal answered.

Bitsy opened the back door to go inside, and Miss Priss slid out while her owner went in. The cat made straight for Lindy and jumped into her lap. She settled with a contented sigh, her head resting on the arm Lindy automatically wrapped around her.

Lindy ran a hand down the cat's soft fur. "Don't tell my kids. Every time the cat food ad comes on—the one with the beautiful white cat—Mike and I are deafened by pleas for one. If they saw Miss Priss, we'd be in deep trouble."

"But don't you already have a bunch of other pets?" Molly asked. She raised a teasing eyebrow. "What's one more?"

"We have a Labrador, a boxer, a guinea pig, and a tank full of fish—a cat would either eat or be eaten."

"I wonder how Miss Priss would like Angus," Molly mused. "They're about the same size."

"No offense to Angus, but I think Miss Priss would put him in his place in about four seconds."

Molly agreed, though she felt slightly disloyal about it. She caught sight of Bitsy at the patio door and hopped up to open it for her.

Bitsy bustled through the doorway with a tray full of colorful glasses, a plate of Scottish shortbread, and pretty floral paper plates and napkins. She set it on the patio table and gestured grandly. "Help yourselves."

"You didn't have to go to all this trouble," Molly said, helping herself to a cookie. "But I'm glad you did." She took a bite of the shortbread and let the buttery goodness melt on her tongue. "You made the shortbread, didn't you? Laura would be very impressed."

"Nobody lives in Loch Mallaig for long without learning to make shortbread. I made it for my staff as a treat for surviving another year with our students, but I can spare a few pieces." Bitsy cocked her head at Lindy. "How are you doing? It can't be easy with your nemesis getting herself killed."

Molly blinked. *She doesn't waste time getting to the point.*

Lindy shrugged. "It's been a strange couple of days."

"Do they have any idea who did it?" Bitsy glanced from Lindy to Molly.

"Not that they've shared with us." Molly briefly pondered whether Bitsy's questions were pushy or just normal curiosity.

Bitsy sighed. "Well, dead end there, but I know you can tell me the Robby MacDuff story. Did he really get hung up on your picket fence?"

The speed with which small town gossip traveled never failed to amaze Molly. "He tried to vault over it, and the leg of his shorts got caught. If it hadn't been for that, he'd have cleared the fence and disappeared into the night like the rest of his friends."

Bitsy stopped with her tea halfway to her mouth. "He wasn't alone? I didn't realize that."

"There were four of them." Molly spread her napkin on her knee. "They ran from Dumfries Park like the zombie apocalypse had come and the undead were on their heels."

Lindy grinned as she ran her hand down Miss Priss's back. "He was so mad they left him. You should have heard him. You'd have put him in detention if he ever used that language at school."

Bitsy assumed her principal's persona. "You're right. I would have. No bad language in my school." She relaxed a bit and nibbled a piece of shortbread. "Robby's an interesting boy. He's clever but also devious. It'll be interesting to see whether his good angel or his bad angel wins out. Sometimes he's a real sweetheart, but other times I can tell his mother's been at him again."

"What do you mean?" Molly thought of the stern woman who had visited the bakery that morning and wondered what simmered beneath the stony surface. "Is she abusive toward Robby?"

"Certainly not," Bitsy said quickly. "She'd never hurt Robby. He's her ticket to celebrity."

Molly paused as she sipped her iced tea. "How's that, exactly?"

Bitsy laughed at Molly's obvious skepticism. "Well you see, Isabella is a great fan of Scottish independence."

"What's that got to do with Robby?" Lindy asked.

"Quite a lot as far as she's concerned," Bitsy said.

"So she's just like the first Isabella MacDuff—in her mind." Molly smiled at Bitsy's surprised expression. "Hamish, my source of all things Scottish, told me Isabella's story from back in the early days of the wars for Scottish independence. William Wallace, *Braveheart,* and all that."

"What Scottish independence?" Lindy frowned, confused. "Scotland's part of the United Kingdom."

"Since 1707," Bitsy agreed. "Still, Scotland has never lost its national identity and traditions. It's sort of like Texas, unique and proud of its individuality while still part of a larger entity. Every so often, there's a renewed call for Scottish independence, and our Isabella is one of the current callers."

"How can she be part of any movement over there when she lives here?" Molly asked.

Lindy reached for another shortbread. "Is she rich or something? Can she underwrite the movement and get special favors because of it?"

"No money, but she does have a game in mind." Bitsy paused dramatically. "She plans to offer Robby for the cause." Molly and Lindy stared blankly until she added, "To be chief of Clan MacDuff."

Molly had to laugh at the thought of Robby wrapped in a plaid with face painted blue, rallying his men with a battle cry. "Do the rest of the MacDuffs know about this?"

Bitsy grinned. "Who can say?"

Lindy appeared fascinated. "So she lives in Loch Mallaig because it's as close to the actual Scotland as she can get without going there. Is that it?"

Molly contemplated everything Bitsy had said. "Somehow our Isabella equates herself with the Isabella of old, only instead of crowning someone king, she'll crown her son the clan's chief."

Bitsy toyed with a paper napkin. "I can always tell the days after she's done her you're-going-to-rule-the-world speech by the way Robby acts. He'll strut around like he's already some powerful clan chief. He's demanding, belittling, and often just plain offensive."

Molly felt sad for the boy. "How does a kid overcome the irrationality of a parent like that?"

"Like I said, good angel versus bad angel." Bitsy shrugged. "In the end, Robby will choose."

"What about his friends?" Lindy was likely thinking about her own son, who was roughly Robby's age. "Don't they give him a hard time when he gets all laird-y and chief-ish?"

Bitsy shrugged. "The way they deserted him last night, they certainly haven't given him the loyalty a chief would get. Not that he should expect it. He's not a chief and they aren't MacDuffs."

"And they're thirteen." Lindy placed her empty iced tea glass on the table. "My son's thirteen. Not a pretty sight a lot of the time."

"Which brings us to one of the reasons we came over," Molly said. "We'd like to speak with Robby and his friends. We were wondering if you could give us their full names and tell us where they live."

"You plan to just show up at their houses?" Bitsy asked, clearly skeptical.

"You could write us a letter of recommendation." Molly said it tongue-in-cheek, but Bitsy took her seriously.

"Better than that." The principal stood abruptly. "I'll come with you."

"You will?" Lindy asked.

"You bet." The women carried the empty glasses and plates inside, then Bitsy led the way to the sidewalk in front of her house. "Maggie Maclay lives right down the street. The others are Ian Commons and Cara Younger."

A few minutes later, the women stood in front of a large but somewhat shabby house. Children's toys were scattered in the too-long grass, and the porch was decorated with trails of muddy footprints that led to a pile of dirty boots. Bitsy pushed a doorbell that echoed faintly inside.

A thirtysomething woman with frizzy hair and a pronounced baby bump appeared on the other side of the screen door. Three little kids of varying heights peered around her to see who had come to call. Before they got a good look, however, a huge St. Bernard pushed his way to the front of the queue and panted at Molly and her friends in greeting, his fluffy tail waving.

The woman's eyes widened when she saw Bitsy. "Ms. Barkley! Is something wrong at school? I hope none of my babies are in trouble."

"Everything's fine at school," Bitsy answered reassuringly. "I didn't mean to upset you, Mrs. Maclay."

Mrs. Maclay relaxed, resting a hand on the head of a little girl who had clearly cut her own bangs recently. "What can I do for you?"

"I'm looking for Maggie. Is she around?"

"Let me check." Mrs. Maclay glanced over her shoulder and hollered, "Anyone seen Maggie?"

"She went to Cara's," answered a young boy's voice.

"Or Ian's." A girl's giggles floated out the door. "She likes Ian."

"Gross," the boy said. "Run, Ian, run! Maggie carries extra-strength girl germs!"

"That's not nice." All traces of the girl's giggles had disappeared. "You're mean!"

A series of thuds and shrieks, both male and female, followed.

"Cara's or Ian's," Mrs. Maclay offered, then turned toward her unseen children. "No fighting! I mean it." She disappeared into the house, trailed by the younger kids and the still happy dog.

Molly sent up a brief prayer of gratitude for her sweet, gentle, quiet Chloe—and little Angus—as the three women turned to leave. "How many children do the Maclays have?" she asked Bitsy.

"Six at last count," Bitsy said, "and apparently there's a seventh on the way. Maggie is the oldest—a nice kid with a strong streak of independence."

"Developed for self-defense," Lindy said.

Bitsy laughed. "I have three of her younger sibs at school now, and then there are two who haven't started kindergarten yet." She gestured toward her house. "We should take a car to go see Ian. His house is closer than Cara's."

"I'll drive," Molly volunteered, and led the way to her silver Honda Fit.

Once inside, Bitsy leaned back in her seat and sighed. "I appreciate my quiet house every time I visit the Maclays. I may spend my day with the youthful masses, but I come home to peace."

"Is Ian's family as large?" Molly asked as she put the car in drive.

"No, not at all. Take a left at the corner," Bitsy said. "In about half a mile you'll turn right. I'll tell you when."

Molly followed Bitsy's directions, grateful she had joined them. Not only was it easier to find the houses, but her presence would make talking to strangers a great deal less awkward.

Bitsy pointed. "The red brick place is Ian's. I wonder if the little Maclay sister was right and we'll find both Ian and Maggie." Bitsy unbuckled her seat belt as Molly slipped the car into park, but she paused before opening her door. "Ian's parents are nice folks. They own a huge lumbering business. They're one of the richest families in town, but you'd never know it. Ian has one younger brother named Liam. Both boys are smart and well-behaved. You'll like Ian."

But they didn't get to meet him.

"I'm sorry, Ms. Barkley," Mrs. Commons said. "Ian's at the baseball field. He's his team's star pitcher." The woman beamed with pride. "I'd be there, but I'm waiting for a plumber to come fix the kitchen sink. This is Ian's last year in the league. Next year he'll age out and move up." Then it seemed to register that the elementary school principal was at her door. With a skeptical glance at Molly and Lindy, she asked, "Is something the matter with Liam?"

Molly realized Liam must be younger than his teenaged brother to still be in Bitsy's elementary school, while Ian would be in middle school.

Bitsy held up a calming hand. "Nothing's wrong, Mrs. Commons. He's doing very well as always. I hear nothing but good things from his teachers."

Mrs. Commons smiled as if this was more what she expected to hear. "I'll tell Ian you were asking for him. Is there a message?"

"That won't be necessary," Bitsy said. "Thanks for your time."

"You know," Mrs. Commons said, "you're the third request for Ian this evening. Cara and Maggie were here, all giggly. I think they both have crushes on him."

"I wouldn't be surprised." Bitsy smiled. "He's a good-looking boy, and nice to boot."

Molly and Lindy started to turn away, but Mrs. Commons stopped them cold with her next words. "The other person looking for Ian made me uncomfortable. It was a man with lots of tattoos. He had two men with him, all tattooed up too." She ran her hands up first one arm, then the other. "I don't like the idea of them seeking out my son."

Molly felt her stomach drop. Why was Rick Capuana asking for Ian? "If it concerns you, Mrs. Commons, I suggest you report it to the police."

"I think that's a good idea," Bitsy added.

Mrs. Commons appeared hesitant. "But the police have that terrible murder to deal with."

"Call the police." Bitsy's voice was principal stern. "They need to be alerted if some unknown adult is asking after minors."

He's not unknown to everyone here, Molly thought with a sideways glance at Lindy.

"When you put it that way . . ." Mrs. Commons pulled her cell phone from her pocket and gave them a distracted wave as she closed the door.

None of the women spoke until they got into Molly's car. Bitsy broke the silence. "Should I assume Mr. Tattoos is Rick Capuana?"

"I'm afraid so," Lindy answered.

"Do you think Capuana has tried to speak to the other kids too?" Molly asked.

"And how did he learn about the kids?" Lindy bit her lip. "I do not trust that man one bit."

"Neither will Chief Thomson or Greer Anderson," Bitsy assured them. "The baseball field is out by the elementary school."

Molly felt nostalgic as they walked up to the bleachers that sat on the first base side of the field. Molly had sat through years of Chloe's soccer games in backless seats just like these. At least the weather was warm and sunny today as opposed to the many days she'd sat shivering in autumns gone by, a fleece blanket wrapped around her legs and her hands jammed in her coat pockets or snuggled in Kevin's larger, warmer hands.

She spotted Maggie and Cara immediately. The ponytail and long fall of blonde hair were enough to identify them, but their calls of, "Come on, Ian!" and "Hit a homer, Ian!" confirmed it.

Molly leaned toward Bitsy. "I take it that's Ian at bat."

"The very same."

Ian was tall and gangly, all elbows and knees. He swung at the ball barreling toward him and missed. The two girls put their heads together and giggled.

"Which is which?" Molly indicated the girls.

"Ponytail is Maggie, long hair is Cara," Bitsy said. "That's Ian's dad in the other dugout. He coaches that team, and Liam plays on it. In fact, he's the catcher squatting behind Ian."

The girl with the long locks—Cara—flipped her hair and turned to survey the bleachers, smiling sweetly as her gaze skimmed over a trio of boys sitting three rows behind her and Maggie.

"I know Cara now that I have a good look at her face," Molly said, surprised. "She and her father come to the bakery every Saturday morning. It's so sweet. They order pastries and something to drink, then get a table and talk. I've been impressed because he really listens to her and they seem to enjoy each other."

After bestowing a smile on the boys behind her, Cara's gaze came to rest on Molly and her companions. The smile disappeared, and an expression of something akin to horror appeared in its place. She spun around and whispered to Maggie, who peeked over her shoulder with the same horrified expression. There was a brief flurry of whispers, then the girls rose and worked their way down the seats to the ground.

In the meantime, Ian swung at a perfect ball and connected with a very impressive *crack*. The ball sailed, and Ian ran the bases to the cheers of the spectators. When the ball disappeared over the fence, he rounded third and headed to home plate, where he was welcomed by the slaps and hugs of his teammates and the ovation of the crowd—everyone but his biggest fans.

Maggie and Cara had disappeared.

12

The game ended with Ian's team losing despite his home run. His little brother and his father on the opposing team were all smiles and good cheer. As the teams shook hands, Ian ignored his dancing brother.

When Bitsy led Molly and Lindy to the teen, he was not happy to see them.

"Hello, Ian." Bitsy beamed at him. "Good game."

He snorted.

"No, it was great," Molly said. "Your home run was wonderful, and your pitching kept them to two points."

Ian was determined not to be cheered. "Not much good when we only got one."

"Ian, this is Mrs. Ferris from Bread on Arrival."

When Bitsy said this, Ian took a step backward, eyeing Molly warily. His distress over the game was replaced by a guarded expression.

Molly made her smile as friendly as she could manage. "I just want to ask you a couple of questions about your midnight outing."

He swallowed, his Adam's apple bobbing. "What midnight outing?" He peeked over his shoulder toward his father.

Molly noted the movement. *So his parents don't know he was out running around with friends instead of sleeping in his bed.* "We know you were with Robby and the girls," she said.

"How could you know that?" He crossed his arms over his chest and stared mutinously. "Since I wasn't there and all."

Molly wondered why denial was so important. "I saw you, Ian, running across my lawn."

"Not me." His voice cracked. He cleared his throat and repeated more forcefully, "Not me."

"If not you, then why did Robby call your name when he got stuck?"

"So you say," Ian muttered.

Molly nodded. "So I say."

Ian merely glared.

"You realize your denial just makes us more curious, don't you?" Molly asked. "Now more than ever we want to know why you won't tell us what happened. Why lie rather than give us the truth?"

Ian shifted his gaze from Molly to Bitsy to Lindy. "I don't know what you're talking about."

"Ian, come on," Mr. Commons called, gesturing for his son. "Time to go."

"Bye," Ian said with a smirk, then bolted.

Bitsy watched him go, astonishment in her expression. "I have never seen Ian so . . ." She seemed at a loss for words.

"So thirteen?" Lindy suggested.

Bitsy gave a little laugh. "Exactly."

Molly glanced around the ball field, which was now nearly deserted. "I think we can safely say none of those kids want to tell us what was going on."

"The blow to my ego is fierce," Lindy said wryly.

"You'll survive." Molly chuckled. "I guess we might as well visit Robby and find out what he's got to say, if anything."

Once in the car, Bitsy said, "You two know Robby, so you don't need me running interference for you there. Would you mind dropping me at home? I've got some work to do for school tomorrow. The end of the year demands so much time."

"Not a problem." Molly pulled out of the parking lot. "We appreciate the help you've given us."

"I do have to say I'm glad I work with elementary school students." Bitsy shook her head, clearly confounded by the teens' behavior. "Hormones haven't kicked in yet with my kids. They're still all curiosity and sweetness."

"It's a wild ride indeed," Lindy said. "My teens put me through the wringer."

When they pulled up at Bitsy's house, the principal unbuckled her seat belt. "I hope you have some luck with Robby. Let me know how it goes."

"We will," Molly said, then exchanged a quick glance with Lindy. At her friend's nod, Molly added, "Lindy and I are going out to dinner with Laura and Carol tomorrow night at the King's Heid Pub. Would you like to join us? We can catch you up then."

Bitsy's face lit up. "I'd love to. What time?"

"Six," Molly answered. "I'll call and add one to our reservation."

After Bitsy closed the door and waved them on their way, Molly and Lindy followed the directions she'd given them to a tidy clapboard house in a cul-de-sac. Yew bushes edged the foundation and a basketball net hung over the garage door.

"I don't expect we'll get much information from Robby," Lindy said as they strode up the walk. "He was awfully belligerent last night."

"But those kids saw something. I know it." Molly rang the doorbell.

The door opened and Mrs. MacDuff appeared, still wearing her clan tartan skirt and thistle brooch. Instead of greeting Molly and Lindy, she merely gazed at them impassively.

"Hello, Mrs. MacDuff," Molly said, discomfited by the woman's expressionless demeanor. "My name is Molly Ferris. I've seen you at Bread on Arrival."

Mrs. MacDuff still said nothing, and her face remained stony. But it was her unblinking silver-eyed stare that iced Molly's spine. Apart from the fact that the irises had changed color from bright blue to a creepy gray, they were vacant, absent of any emotion.

Molly cleared her throat. "May we see Robby?"

Finally an expression touched Isabella MacDuff's face—wariness. "Robby? Why?"

"We'd like to ask him some questions," Molly explained, trying not to stumble over her words. "He was at the bakery last night, and I'd like to ask him if he saw anything unusual."

"Last night?"

"Yes." Molly didn't want to get Robby in trouble by telling the specific time, but she knew it wouldn't be long before it came out.

Mrs. MacDuff's silver eyes narrowed. "You're not open at night. Why would you think you'd seen him there?"

"Because we did," Lindy answered.

Without acknowledging Lindy's presence, Mrs. MacDuff straightened her shoulders, ferocity coming into her expression. "Are you aware that I am the namesake of a famous woman?"

Despite wondering where that comment came from, Molly nodded. "I know a little about the original Isabella MacDuff."

"She was the Countess of Buchan as a result of her forced marriage to a man who was loyal to the English. Can you imagine a forced marriage?" Mrs. MacDuff appeared outraged on historic Isabella's behalf.

"It's hard for us to imagine such a thing today," Molly said, "but back then wealthy or noble families used marriage as a means of forming alliances. Love wasn't a consideration."

"She was a Scottish patriot," the present-day Isabella declared.

"Yes I know," Molly said. "She crowned Robert the Bruce King of Scotland."

"The English captured her." Mrs. MacDuff was clearly disgusted at the notion. "They saw her as a traitor."

"How very sad." Molly's discomfort was turning into impatience. *What does this have to do with asking Robby a couple of questions about last night?*

"They hung her in an iron cage from the castle walls at Berwick-upon-Tweed for four years," Mrs. MacDuff continued. "Four years! She hung there in all kinds of weather."

Molly had to admit the iron cage was more than a bit creepy. "Those old kings knew how to mete out punishment, didn't they?"

"As her namesake, I must strive to be as brave as she. So I must say no."

Molly thought she knew what Isabella was saying, but she had to be sure. "No to what?"

"No to you bothering my Robby. I must protect him. He will be our clan's chief in a few years, and I must keep him safe, even if I must deal with an iron cage."

For a moment Molly had no words. Finally she managed, "I'm not a danger to Robby, Mrs. MacDuff."

The imposing woman merely shrugged. She took a step back and, without another word, closed the door.

Lindy stared at Molly in disbelief. "She just shut the door in our faces."

Molly stared at the slab of wood in amazement. "She did."

With apparently nothing else to be done, they started back toward the car.

Before she opened the car door, Lindy peered back at the house. She froze. "Molly," she murmured. "Second floor, last window on the left."

Molly glanced up. Robby MacDuff was looking down at them with a huge smile on his face. He waved, then backed away, clearly laughing as he went.

When her alarm went off on Thursday, Molly felt almost normal, having finally gotten a good night's sleep. Hoping not to wake Lindy, she dressed quickly, fed Angus and let him out, then headed downstairs.

After prepping the front of the house for the day ahead, she went to the kitchen to whip up a batch of shortbread for Guid Nychburris Day. While she worked, she pondered all she had learned about Janae Harbison and her past life as Alana Gladstone. But by the time several pans of cookies were ready for the oven, she had no more answers to the murder today than she had yesterday.

Molly had just set the timer when Bridget peeked into the kitchen. "There's someone here to see you, Molly."

Molly glanced at the clock. The bakery had only been open a few minutes. Who could be asking for her this early? "Be right there." She placed the magnetic timer on the oven door. "Carol, can you please pull these out if I'm not back in time?"

"Sure." Carol waved her hand. "Go see who it is."

When Molly stepped into the café, Bridget pointed to a girl with a waterfall of long, blonde hair huddled at one of the tables. With a nod of thanks to Bridget, Molly approached Cara Younger and sat down in the chair across from her.

Cara had circles under her eyes, and she appeared to be a breath away from either bolting or hyperventilating. Maybe both.

Molly did her best to break the ice gently. "You came without your dad this morning?" The answer was so obvious Cara didn't say anything. Molly rested her folded hands on the table. "I like seeing you come in here with him. So many kids don't spend quality time with their parents."

"He travels with his job, so he says that's how he keeps track of me." Cara issued a small smile. "I'm an only child."

"My daughter is too. Her name's Chloe, and she lives in Milwaukee. She's a veterinarian."

"Really? Doesn't that take a lot of studying?" Cara seemed to be relaxing a little.

"She went to college, then veterinary school after that. It took a long time, but it was worth it."

"Does she like big animals or small ones?"

"I think she likes whichever one needs her help."

"I think I'd like small ones, like your dog. I've seen him around. He's cute."

"Thank you."

Silence fell. Whatever Cara had come to say, she was having difficulty getting it out.

Molly indicated the display cases. "Would you like something to eat?"

Cara's eyes went wide. "I don't have any money with me. I was so nervous about coming that I forgot."

"Don't worry about the cost," Molly said. "I have an in with the owner."

Cara seemed confused by Molly's joke. "You are the owner, aren't you? My dad said you were. Last night at the game I recognized you from seeing you on Saturdays. That's why I came here."

"You're right. I'm one of the owners. My partners are in the kitchen baking."

"It always smells so good in here."

"It does, doesn't it? What's your favorite pastry to get when you come in with your dad?"

"I like the hot cross buns with the icing crosses on top, but you don't have them all the time."

"Our chief baker rotates items, but you're in luck. We have them today. I think they go well with a cup of tea. Or would you rather have a glass of milk?"

For a moment Cara was undecided, but she came down on the side of adulthood. "Tea, please."

Molly rose and busied herself getting two cups of English breakfast tea. She watched Cara as the girl alternately darted her gaze around the bakery and stared at her own hands. Maybe it would be best to just ask outright why she'd come.

After Molly set down the tea and hot cross buns, Cara put three packets of sugar in her tea. She noticed Molly watching and blushed. "I like sweet things."

"Nothing wrong with that," Molly said. "But it's very hot, so be careful."

Cara took a tiny sip. She made a face and put the cup down. "It is."

Molly kept an eye on customer traffic while they ate their hot cross buns, but although the stream was steady, it was nothing Bridget couldn't handle. Still, it was time to get Cara talking.

"Do you want to tell me why you came, Cara?" Molly asked. "I don't think it was for breakfast."

Cara stared at her lap. "It's hard."

"Is it about the other night?"

The girl's head snapped up, her eyes huge and worried. "We made a pact."

"Who made a pact?" Molly asked, though she knew full well who.

"Me, Maggie, Ian, and Robby."

"What was the pact?"

Cara bit her lip. "We wouldn't tell the police."

Molly had expected that answer, but she was still surprised to hear it stated so plainly. She took care to not let criticism color her voice. "And you're here because I'm not the police?"

"Yeah. But I'm still breaking the intent of the pact."

"And that bothers you."

"A lot. They're my friends. They're going to be so mad."

"Let me ask a question," Molly said. "Was it a wise pact to make?"

Cara took a deep breath. "We were all scared, you know? First, we didn't want our parents to know." Tears glistened in her eyes. "My dad will be so disappointed."

"Does he have reason to be disappointed? Did you do anything wrong?"

"I snuck out," Cara squeaked, clearly devastated by her admission.

"Besides that, I mean. Did you hurt anyone's property? Did you take anything that wasn't yours?"

"No!" Cara cried out, then glanced at the nearby customers noticing her and lowered her voice. "We didn't do anything but run around. Mostly we giggled and joked about being afraid someone was hiding behind the pine trees."

Molly could picture them, four kids on an adventure, impressed at their own audacity.

"Robby bet us all we didn't have the courage to sneak out," Cara continued, "but we did. We met at midnight and mostly it was sort of fun, being out when no one else was." Her face brightened as she remembered, and then guilt clouded her expression. "Except we weren't the only ones out after all."

"Tell me about it, Cara. What did you see?"

Cara checked her watch. "I-I have to go. I'm going to be late for school." She reached for the backpack resting on the floor beside her.

Molly channeled her long-dormant mom voice. "Cara."

The girl sighed and dropped her bag. "We went into Dumfries Park. We were going to sneak up to Crag Mallaig to see if anyone was there, you know, like couples kissing or something."

"I've heard that goes on over there."

"At first we didn't hear anything." Cara lifted her head, her face intent. "Then we heard someone yelling. Ian and I wanted to run, but Maggie and Robby didn't. So we all stayed. All for one, you know?"

Except when Robby got held up on the fence. Molly didn't comment, though.

"We sneaked up on one side of Crag Mallaig, and somebody else, more than one person, was on the other side. We couldn't see them, and they couldn't see us. We could only hear them, mostly because of the yelling." Cara took a quick sip of her tea as if it would give her courage. "I mean, it was scary hearing someone shouting. 'No more!' he yelled. 'No more! Leave me alone or else!'"

"It was a man yelling?" Molly clarified.

"I think so."

Molly took a moment to sympathize with this young girl, who on a lark had come upon something quite terrifying.

"Then there was a big noise—bang!—like someone had fired a gun." Fear suddenly lit Cara's eyes, and her frightened gaze pleaded with Molly.

Molly immediately understood what the girl needed. "Janae Harbison wasn't shot. You didn't hear her being killed."

"You're sure?"

"I'm sure."

Cara released a great sigh, and her shoulders relaxed. "That makes me feel so much better."

"So you ran when you heard the bang?" Molly asked.

But Cara shook her head. "We sort of froze, you know? You don't expect to hear a gunshot in the middle of the night. Or ever, really. When someone came running toward us from the road, we stayed hidden in the shadows of the rocks."

"Was that the man who was yelling?"

"No, he must have run in the other direction. The person who ran past us was a woman. She was carrying something that looked like a baseball bat."

A chill swept over Molly, raising all the hairs on her arms and neck. These kids might not have heard Janae murdered, but they may well have seen or heard the murderer. "You have to speak to the police, honey. You can't keep something this important from them."

"I thought maybe you could tell them for me," Cara said. "Then I won't be breaking the pact. And my parents won't know."

Molly reached out and covered the girl's cold hand. "Cara . . ."

The girl sighed as if her life was coming to an end. "I know. But I hate to tell on Ms. Barkley. I always liked her."

13

Molly startled at Cara's words. Bitsy Barkley? Whatever Molly had expected, this wasn't it. When she finally caught her breath, she peered at Cara. "You're sure you saw Ms. Barkley with a bat?"

Cara nodded. "I'm sure. It's not like anyone else looks like her." She held her hand out as if measuring Bitsy's lack of stature.

No wonder none of the kids wanted to speak with them last evening. The sight of Bitsy asking questions must have scared them to death.

"I'm going to call the police now." After one more reassuring pat on Cara's hand, Molly pulled out her phone and dialed Greer. "I have someone you need to speak to. Can you come to the bakery?"

"I can be there as soon as I get dressed for work," Greer replied.

Molly watched Cara nervously toy with a lock of blonde hair. "Maybe skip that for now."

"You mean no uniform?" Greer sounded intrigued. "You must have a Nervous Nellie."

"I do."

"Huh. I'll be there in ten."

"See you then." Molly disconnected the call. "Cara, what's your mom's phone number? Or your dad's?"

"You're calling my parents?" The teen's voice was a squeak of distress.

"One of them needs to be present while you talk to Officer Anderson."

"I don't mind talking without them."

Molly raised an eyebrow. "Officer Anderson will mind."

"My dad's out of town and won't be home until dinnertime. You'll have to talk to my mom." Cara turned pleading eyes to Molly. "Can't we leave her out of it? You can be my adult present."

Molly shook her head. It was time to get Mrs. Younger involved.

Cara let her head fall forward until it thudded on the table. "When Mom and Dad hear about this, I'm going to be grounded for life."

Molly bit back a smile at the girl's dramatics as she dialed and greeted Mrs. Younger. After some initial suspicion, the woman agreed to come to the bakery as soon as possible.

After putting her phone away, Molly pointed at Cara's empty plate. "Want another bun?"

Cara fidgeted, then blurted, "I don't want to get in trouble. I came because I wanted to help but didn't want to upset my parents. And now?" Her voice trembled slightly.

Molly patted Cara's hand. "Sometimes doing what's right is hard, but it's still right."

Cara didn't appear convinced.

Molly rose and got Bridget's attention. "Could you plate up two more hot cross buns, please? No, make that four. We might as well have Greer's and Mrs. Younger's waiting for them."

Cara slumped in her chair. "I should have kept my mouth shut."

Business continued all around them as the workers setting up booths and displays for Guid Nychburris Day came in for coffee and sustenance. Some of the out-of-town vendors had been in Loch Mallaig for a few days already, so Molly recognized a few familiar faces and looked forward to seeing their booths set up at the festival.

The one-day event would take place in the park and along the lake, and the stretch of Yooper Boulevard that ran by the park would be closed to traffic so people could walk safely. The entertainers, including The Leaping Lowlanders, would perform by the public pier. People would bring their chairs and settle in for a fun afternoon of singers and dancers.

Greer and Mrs. Younger arrived amid the hustle and bustle of customer traffic, and quickly settled around the table with Cara and Molly. An unhappy Cara repeated for the newcomers what she had told Molly. The girl's eyes filled with tears at the shock on her mother's face when she confessed to sneaking out to meet her friends.

When Cara was finished with her story, Greer smiled encouragingly. "It was brave of you to come forward, Cara."

Cara's cheeks turned pink at the praise, and she snuck a peek at her mother.

Mrs. Younger, recovered from her shock, hugged her daughter. "I'm proud of you for doing what was right even though you knew it could get you in trouble."

Cara grimaced. "Are you and Dad going to ground me forever?"

"We'll let you know." But Mrs. Younger's expression was warm and loving.

"I'll write up all you've just said," Greer told Cara. "Tomorrow I'd like you to come to the station to check the statement and make sure I have it right. Then you can either make corrections or sign it."

Cara appeared forlorn. "Everybody will know I told."

Greer patted the girl's hand. "If it makes you feel any better, I heard from a colleague that Ian Commons and his father showed up at the station while I was on my way here."

Cara's expression was hopeful for the first time. "Ian's telling too?"

Greer nodded, and Cara sagged in relief, then she and her mother quickly left the bakery so that Cara wouldn't be late to school.

After watching the front door shut, Molly turned back to Greer.

"Bitsy Barkley in the woods with a baseball bat?" She pulled a face. "It sounds like the solution to a game of Clue."

Greer shrugged. "There's a big difference between Bitsy with a baseball bat and Bitsy using that bat to kill someone."

"You didn't find a bat at the scene?"

Greer raised an eyebrow. "You know I can't talk about an open case."

"So you did find the bat?"

"I didn't say that."

"So you didn't find the bat." Molly stacked the dirty cups and plates on their table. "It can only be one or the other."

"If you say so. See you around." With a wave, Greer left.

If Molly were a betting woman, she'd lay odds that a bat hadn't been found. Did that mean Bitsy had taken it home with her after she'd used it? *If* she'd used it.

Molly pictured the little principal with her cozy blue house and cuddly cat. What she couldn't picture was that same person swinging a lethal bat at a woman in the woods.

Lost in thought, Molly cleared and cleaned the tables. When she straightened and turned toward the kitchen, she nearly gasped. Isabella MacDuff stood so close behind her that Molly would have bumped into her if she'd taken another step.

Instead, Molly edged a few inches away, noting that today the woman's eyes were blue, though just as flat as when they had been silver. She wore a navy shirt and plaid slacks. Another of the MacDuff tartans? Either way, the outfit was rather unflattering.

"Mrs. MacDuff," Molly said in greeting. "How are you today?"

Mrs. MacDuff didn't answer. She merely stared at Molly. Was she trying to be intimidating?

If so, it's working. Molly shifted from one foot to the other. "May I help you in some way?"

Finally, the woman spoke. "I've come to ask why you felt it necessary to come to my house and seek out my son. I don't want to have to tell the police that you are harassing us."

Harassing? Molly felt a rush of anger at the accusation. She took a breath to calm herself. "I had a few questions I wanted to ask Robby about Tuesday night. I really don't think that qualifies as harassment."

Mrs. MacDuff cocked her head as if she didn't quite understand Molly. "Why would you want to ask him about Tuesday evening?"

"Not evening. Night."

Mrs. MacDuff returned to her silent staring.

"You see . . ." Molly paused. Then she wondered why she was so hesitant about getting Robby in trouble with his mother. Given his attitude toward life in general and Molly in particular, the kid deserved some trouble. *Just spit it out, Molly.* "Robby was here Tuesday night."

"No, he was not. He was at home. We watched TV together until he went to bed."

"He was here much later than bedtime. It was after one o'clock."

"In the morning?" Mrs. MacDuff's eyes went wide and her face turned pale. "Y'all must be mistaken. I saw him go to bed."

"I was having difficulty sleeping and was sitting in my chair by the window," Molly told her. "I saw Robby come running from Dumfries Park right toward this place." She indicated the bakery. "He got to our back fence and tried to jump over it. The leg of his shorts got caught and he was stuck. I had to go down and free him."

"That was when she was killed." Mrs. MacDuff grabbed the table for support.

Molly felt a rush of sympathy in spite of herself. No mother wanted her child near a murder, no matter how peripherally. "I thought he might have seen something," she said gently. "That's why I wanted to speak to him."

"Y'all must be mistaken," she repeated. "He couldn't have seen somethin'. He wasn't there." Mrs. MacDuff said the word *there* as though it had two syllables, and Molly wondered fleetingly where the woman had lived before coming to Loch Mallaig.

"He could be a big help to the police, Mrs. MacDuff. And it would be a good way for him to show his leadership qualities."

"He'd be no help whatsoever because he wasn't there." *There* had only one syllable that time. Mrs. MacDuff had regained control of her accent. "Let me repeat. He. Wasn't. There."

"Mrs. MacDuff, you must—"

"You leave him alone." The woman's blue eyes blazed. "He's a very sensitive boy." Then, still pale and unsteady on her feet, Mrs. MacDuff left the bakery without another word.

Molly was still reeling from the bizarre conversation when Lindy came charging into the room. She grasped Molly by the elbow, making the plates Molly still clutched rattle.

"I need you, Molly," Lindy said urgently. "We have to go back to the scene of the crime."

14

"Why are we doing this?" Molly asked as she followed Lindy into the park and toward Crag Mallaig.

"Why not?" her friend answered.

Plainly visible encircling the rocks ahead, the yellow police tape proclaiming *Crime Scene Keep Out* seemed to Molly a good reason why not.

Lindy grabbed Molly's hand and pulled her along. "It was dark when we were here before. I want to see things in the light. Maybe we'll notice something important."

"Something the police missed? I don't think so."

Lindy shrugged. "I don't really think so either, but I have to be thorough anyway. I'm trying to establish my innocence, remember?"

"No one's suggested you're guilty."

"That doesn't mean they don't think it. I need to be squeaky clean for Skye. I want her to trust me."

Molly nodded. That was a reason she could understand.

When they came to the yellow tape, the women exchanged glances, peeked over their shoulders, then ducked under.

"I wonder if the kids felt this reckless the other night." Molly shivered at their illicit behavior. "I'll have a guilty conscience for days."

"Wimp," Lindy teased.

"Big time."

They walked to the place where Janae had lain dead, and a hush fell as they stared at the tragic spot. Molly's stomach tumbled uncomfortably as she thought of what had happened here, and then as she thought of Bitsy with a bat.

"Someone washed away the blood." Lindy pointed. "There wasn't a lot. It wasn't the kind of wound that bled copiously. Still, you'd never know if you didn't know."

"And you know, don't you?" The voice was deep and mocking.

The women spun. When Molly saw Rick Capuana walking—no, sauntering—toward them, her stomach's tumbling turned to churning. His black T-shirt, black jeans, and black boots were what a movie's costume department might dream up for a sinister villain. The tattoo sleeves and mirrored sunglasses compounded the look, as did a big, silver belt buckle with a skull and crossbones on it. His two bodyguards, also dressed all in black, followed a few feet behind.

"So this is the scene of the crime, eh?" Capuana pulled off his sunglasses and ran his gaze over the ground, the formation of rocks, and the surrounding trees. "And you two found her. A fortuitous turn of events, eh, Lindy?" His words dripped with both sarcasm and irony.

"No." Lindy's voice was cold enough to freeze Loch Mallaig.

"We didn't really *find* her," Molly felt compelled to explain. "We responded to the cries of the woman who did."

Capuana nodded. "Verna, right? Alana's roommate and business partner."

Molly nearly recoiled at Capuana's knowledge. In his short time in Loch Mallaig, the man had collected lots of information.

"Up pretty late, weren't you?" He smirked.

Neither Molly nor Lindy said anything. At that moment, Molly realized what it was about him that bothered her so much—besides his corrupt character and evil vibe, of course. It was his air of condescension. He thought he was better than they were, and he was lowering himself to have a conversation with them. Offended, she stiffened her backbone.

Capuana paced back and forth in front of the rocks. "Here's what I want to know: what was she doing here in the middle of the night?"

Even if she knew the answer, Molly wouldn't have told him.

"I can guarantee you one thing." His voice was full of contempt. "She was up to no good. She was a conniving liar and manipulator, and whatever she was doing was as twisted as she was."

Gee, tell me what you really think of her. "What do you believe she was doing?" Molly asked.

"Don't know." He pushed his sunglasses up on his bald head and all but growled in frustration. "Extortion? Blackmail? Drugs? She sure wasn't dancing."

Molly remembered watching Janae demonstrate the Highland fling at class and shook her head sadly. *All that talent in such a deeply flawed woman.*

Capuana kept talking, lining up what he knew. "She might as well have issued invitations, there were so many people here. There was the man who fired the shot, the woman with the bat, and the kids." He glared at Lindy. "Oh, and thanks for setting the cops on me for trying to talk to them."

Lindy glared right back. "We never talked to the police about you and the kids."

"So it was one of the mothers who called the cops," he said. "But you put her up to it, I'm sure. All my troubles always go back to you and your family."

Lindy crossed her arms in a defiant stance. "I'd say it's the other way around."

"That mom who spoke to the police was already upset when we visited her," Molly clarified, again feeling compelled to keep peace with the dangerous felon in their midst. "You have to admit that an unknown man trying to talk to a bunch of minors sets off alarms."

"I never hurt a kid in my life." Capuana seemed genuinely offended that Lindy, Molly, or Mrs. Commons would suspect he had. "I've got standards. All I wanted to know was what they saw."

"You wanted to know if they saw you," Lindy said.

"Me?" He pointed at himself. "How could they see me? I wasn't here."

Molly stared at Lindy. What was she doing, provoking this criminal? He was not a man to challenge. He might not hurt kids, but adults were fair game, and he had his own definition of fair.

"You were in Loch Mallaig," Lindy shot back. "We know that. Why not here too?" She pointed to the ground beneath her feet. "The kids heard a man's voice. Yours? They heard a gunshot. You or one of your goons?" She indicated the two bodyguards standing expressionless mere feet away.

Molly put a hand on Lindy's arm. "Stop baiting the tiger," she said softly.

Lindy kept her eyes on Capuana even as she spoke to Molly. "You're afraid of him?"

"Definitely." Molly's heart beat like a drum in her ears.

Capuana made a disgusted noise. "I'm not going to hurt you. You think I'm stupid enough to do something and end up back in the pen? I'm just trying to find out who to thank for getting rid of my problem."

Molly's gaze went to the huge mass of Crag Mallaig, which stood between them and anyone else around. Rick Capuana could do whatever he wanted to them, and nobody would know. Not that she'd point that out to him.

"How did you find out about the kids?" Molly asked, trying to steer the conversation away from whether or not this man intended to harm her and Lindy.

"Gossip flows freely at the Hiegate Hostelry." Rick slapped at one arm. "What are those little bugs? They bite!"

"Black flies," Molly said. "You should have been here last month. They're pretty much gone now."

Capuana rubbed his arm where he'd been bitten, drawing Molly's eyes to his tattoo. She realized it was a dragon with multicolored scales, wings spread, flying down his arm, ready to eat a cowering woman right above his wrist. She glanced at his other arm and saw a red, blue, and green snake, fangs exposed, slithering through a garden. An animal of uncertain origin waited to be killed. There was no doubt that Rick saw himself as a predator.

"That kid Robby—the dummy who got stuck on your fence—he came over to the motel and was telling the girl behind the desk about his adventures, bragging like he was a big man." Capuana rolled his eyes. "I heard him, and we had a little private conversation, him and me. Did you know he fancies himself some big something or other over in Scotland? Does Scotland even know he exists?"

"I've had occasion to wonder that myself," Molly muttered.

Capuana spread his arms, oozing innocence. "So as you can see, all I was trying to do was check Robby's tale. Like I said, I don't hurt kids."

"Hurray for you," Lindy huffed. She stuffed her hands in the pockets of her jeans, and Molly noted with surprise that they were shaking. For all her bravado, Lindy was scared. Was her breathing becoming labored? Did she have her inhaler with her just in case?

"You don't hurt kids. You only hurt good guys who disagree with you." Lindy's voice vibrated with hostility.

"How many times do I have to tell you? I didn't kill your brother!" Capuana's anger was more than a match for Lindy's. "Like I don't hurt kids, I don't kill guys I got no reason to kill."

Molly blinked. Was he saying he did kill guys he had reason to?

"Then who did kill him?" Lindy cried. "He didn't accidentally fall off that building, and he certainly didn't jump. Somebody pushed him. If it wasn't you, then who?"

Capuana cocked an eyebrow and gazed pointedly at the place where Janae had lain.

Lindy took a step backward and dropped abruptly onto the rock where Molly had sat with Verna two nights earlier. "Alana killed Nate? But he loved her."

Capuana shrugged. "But she didn't love him, and he wouldn't let her go."

"He wanted to save her."

"She didn't want saving."

Lindy's immense sigh was slightly ragged around the edges. "So what happened? Tell me your version."

"It's not my version," Capuana said. "It's the truth."

Molly couldn't help wondering if he'd know the truth if it bit him, but she listened to his story all the same.

"Picture this. I'm at Alana's, this old apartment building," he began. "We're up on the roof where there are some chairs for sitting in the sun. He comes to see her, your brother does. He goes slightly nuts when he finds me on the roof relaxing. The guys are there too." He pointed to the bodyguards. "They aren't going to let him upstairs, but I say it's okay. I figure I'll let him say his piece, then forget about him. When Alana realizes he's there, she says he's driving her crazy and she's not talking to him. She hides behind some big vent."

Molly tore her gaze from Capuana to check on Lindy. She was listening intently, her eyes glassy with tears.

"He pleads with me to leave Alana alone." Capuana shook his head at the memory. "I tell him she isn't worth his pain and worry. I tell him I didn't make her hang around with me. I tell him she chose me and all that went with me."

As the man talked, Molly could picture what happened that long-ago day. A frantic Nate trying to save the girl he loved. Capuana brushing him off, treating him like he was as significant as a fly buzzing around his head. She could imagine the brutal words that Capuana must have used.

Present-day Rick Capuana ran a hand over his bald head. "I tell him to get lost, that Alana's a big girl and makes her own choices. It's not my fault she chose what I offered instead of him. I say he should forget her and find someone nice like him." He said nice as if it was an insult.

Lindy's face contorted with grief and tears poured down her face. Molly's heart broke for her, and she walked to her and stood close, trying to offer strength and comfort.

Capuana frowned. "Why couldn't he see her for what she was? She was a user, not only of pills but of people. All that love he lavished on her? She didn't deserve any of it. She certainly couldn't return it."

"At least I agree with you on that," Lindy said, her voice little more than a whisper. She coughed a few times.

"So I try to get him to leave. I do." It seemed important to Capuana that Lindy believed him, as if this one good deed overrode all the bad stuff. "I keep thinking Alana's gonna pop out of her hiding place and go off on him. She had a terrible temper and didn't mind screaming in your face. He's practically bleeding to death from a broken heart as it is, so I don't want her doing her thing. I never saw anybody so—I don't know—so *committed* to trying to help someone, and it gave me hives, let me tell you."

"He loved her," Lindy choked.

Capuana shook his head. "He was an idiot. I know he was your brother and all, but he was not rational about Alana. So anyway, while he's pleading with me to leave her alone, she pops out of her hiding place just like I feared and comes over to where we're standing. Surprises both of us. I don't know why she didn't stay hidden, but she didn't. She'd have done us all a favor if she had."

Molly tried to imagine what Nate thought when he saw Alana walking toward him. Did he think she had finally recognized that the stability and love he offered were what she needed instead of the dangerous lifestyle she had with Capuana? Or did the fact that she'd been hiding and listening break his heart yet again?

"She wraps herself around my arm and leans in." Capuana demonstrated. "Sort of an I'm-with-him move. She starts telling him to leave her alone, to get out of her life, and that she doesn't want to see him ever again. She walks over to him and starts poking him with her finger." He stabbed his index finger in the air. "She's moving forward and he's moving backward and I'm enjoying the show. I mean, it's funny. This angry little girl versus a big teddy bear guy."

Lindy listened intently, but Molly worried about her. She had wanted to know what happened for years, but finally knowing it had to be bittersweet. Tears continued to stream. She coughed several times and pressed her hand to her chest.

Molly watched Lindy pick up her purse and search for her inhaler. "That's enough, Rick," she said firmly, worrying that hearing his story wasn't good for her friend anymore.

He didn't seem to hear. "She's pushing him closer and closer to the edge, sort of guiding him to where it's crumbling. I don't say anything because I figure she knows what she's doing. It's her roof and all. But she doesn't see or she doesn't care." Capuana shook his head. "Either way, she gets him right up against the low wall that edges the building, right where it's broken. It's an old building, and the wall's low even without crumbling. His legs are against the wall, getting him at the knees, and she's still screaming and poking. He's trying to grab her flailing arms, and she slaps at him and pushes him away."

Lindy gave a little cry and dropped her head to her hands, eyes closed as if to block the mental picture.

Capuana continued animatedly. "He's grabbing for something to hold on to as he starts to fall, but she's the only thing there. She steps back, and in sort of slow motion he goes over backward. His feet were scraping the ground but his shoes were fancy and he slipped all over the place. The last I saw was his shiny black shoes disappear. So I run over and look, and there he is, lying in the side alley. I know right away. Nobody twisted up like that lives."

A wheezing Lindy finally had her inhaler in her hand, and she put it to her mouth and squeezed. Nothing happened. She shook it and tried again as she gasped for air.

Capuana spread his hands, apparently unaware of Lindy's struggles. "So you see? It wasn't me."

Lindy held up her inhaler and turned frantic eyes on Molly. "Help!" she managed. "Empty!"

15

Molly's own breath caught for a moment before she flipped into crisis management mode. "Do you have another one?"

"Always have . . . another." Lindy fished in her purse and pulled out a second inhaler.

Capuana finally realized Lindy was struggling. "What's wrong with her?" he asked Molly.

Molly patted her chest. "Bronchial spasms."

"What? Why?" Capuana and his bodyguards took several steps back.

They watched as Lindy shook her new inhaler, shooting wary glances at her as if they expected her to spontaneously combust. Obviously they'd never known anyone with asthma. If Lindy hadn't been so preoccupied, she would have enjoyed the fact that she'd incapacitated three criminals with her breathing problems.

Capuana pointed at Lindy but spoke to Molly. "I don't know what's wrong, but if she dies, make sure you tell them I didn't kill her."

Molly stared at him, disgusted. "That's your main concern?"

His expression became defensive. "I got accused falsely before. I'm touchy about it happening again."

Lindy put her inhaler in her mouth and pressed as she took a breath.

"That going to fix it?" Capuana asked.

"It should," Molly answered, growing more aggravated with him by the moment. "Your story prompted an asthma attack."

"I said something to make her sick? I got that kind of power?"

He appeared quite pleased with himself now that he knew Lindy wasn't going to die.

Her breathing coming under control, Lindy managed a ragged, "Pig."

He scowled fiercely at her. "Your brother was nicer."

"Probably."

"Can I catch what you got?"

Lindy rolled her eyes.

"I take that as a no. Still . . ." Capuana snapped his fingers, and he and his men faded away, vanishing as if they'd never been there.

Molly sat beside Lindy and put an arm around her shoulder. "You should have said you have leprosy and are highly contagious."

"They'd probably have believed me."

"Would that have been a bad thing?"

Lindy smiled. "Do you have a pharmacy in your lovely little town?" She put her working inhaler back in her bag. She held the empty one in her hand.

"MacPhee's Family Drugstore," Molly said. "It's just down Tattie Bogle Road from the bakery."

"I've been meaning to ask ever since I got your address. What on earth is a tattie bogle? Something Scottish, I'm sure."

"It's a scarecrow in a potato field."

"Do they have any tattie bogles on Tattie Bogle Road?"

Molly laughed, relaxing at Lindy's return to her normal sardonic self. "Not that I've ever seen."

Lindy gasped dramatically, but it was in jest instead of a by-product of her previous peril. "You should organize a community event to correct that deficiency. You can have contests to see who can build the best scarecrow or who can cook the best neeps and tatties."

Molly was pleased at Lindy's ideas, not because she particularly wanted to have such contests but because it was proof she was feeling better. "You've been in the event-planning business much too long," she teased.

"Maybe," Lindy said. "Let's go over to Potato Scarecrow Road so I can get another inhaler. I feel too vulnerable with only one."

"Are you okay to walk back to the house, or should I get the car and come for you?"

"I'm fine now, at least physically. Emotionally?" Lindy wobbled her hand back and forth. "I need to think about what Rick told us."

With a final shoulder squeeze, Molly stood up and began leading the way to the pharmacy. "Are you glad you know what really happened?"

"Yes, assuming he told the truth. He is, after all, a liar and a thief."

"I think he was being honest in this case," Molly said. "He was recounting the story as he remembers it."

"That's my thought too," Lindy agreed. "But what struck me most was that if the police knew what he told us, I'd have an even stronger motive for killing Alana."

"Lindy!" That idea had never crossed Molly's mind.

"Just trying to be realistic," Lindy said.

"But I'm your witness," Molly said firmly. "I know you didn't find out the truth about Nate's death until half an hour ago."

"I appreciate the support, but there's no way you could know for certain when I found out."

Molly couldn't argue with that, and they remained mostly quiet the rest of the way to the drugstore. Once they reached MacPhee's, Molly and Lindy went to the pharmacy counter at the back of the store.

"May I help you?" Cameron MacPhee, the pharmacist, appeared from behind a tall shelf of large plastic containers. The tall, fiftysomething man with a balding pate wore a pressed white lab coat and a pleasant smile.

"I need a refill, please," Lindy said as she held out her inhaler to him.

Cameron checked the label, then indicated a pair of chairs near a blood pressure machine. "You can wait there while I call this in to your doctor's office. It should only be a couple of minutes."

Instead of sitting, Lindy chose to wander the aisles, occasionally sniffing shampoo or checking the nutrition information on a box of protein bars. Molly followed in her wake, and they eventually stopped in the greeting card aisle.

"Don't you think drugstores are fascinating? You need it, they've got it," Lindy said as she picked up a birthday card that had a cartoon moose riding a roller coaster on the front. She opened the card and laughed, then read the message to Molly. "'Hope your birthday is full of amoosement.'"

"Good one," Molly answered, then picked up a card with a cat wearing a birthday hat on the front.

They read cards back and forth for a few minutes. Molly was laughing at a particularly funny one involving three silly pigs when she heard sharp footsteps in the next aisle moving purposefully to the pharmacy counter at the back of the store. Molly glanced down her own aisle and saw Bitsy Barkley stop under the *Pick Up* sign. The principal was in professional mode, wearing a white tunic, navy slacks, and white pumps that gave her petite frame an extra inch. She had a large nautical-striped tote looped over her arm.

Molly started to wave a greeting, then realized Bitsy probably wouldn't see her. She took a few steps but stopped before she reached the end of the aisle. Somehow getting medicine suddenly seemed too private a transaction to interrupt. She'd wait until Bitsy had her prescription and then say hello.

A pharmacy assistant came forward. "Hey, Ms. Barkley. How are you?"

Bitsy smiled at the young woman. "I'm doing fine, Sasha. Still studying at Superior Bay College?"

"I'm graduating soon, then going to pharmacology school."

"That is very impressive. I'm so proud of you." Bitsy patted Sasha's hand. "I'm here for my refill."

Sasha turned to the bins of little white bags arranged in alphabetical order and flipped through the Bs for Barkley. She checked a second time.

"There's nothing here, Ms. Barkley," Sasha said. "Let me check with Dr. MacPhee."

Sasha disappeared for a moment, then reappeared with Cameron in tow. "I'm sorry, Bitsy," he said, his face serious. "Dr. Madison wouldn't renew your prescription."

Bitsy's own face turned scarlet, though Molly couldn't tell if it was from anger or embarrassment. Bitsy straightened her spine. "And why not? He's always done so before."

A visibly uncomfortable Cameron cast a quick glance at Molly, who was trying to look like she wasn't eavesdropping. She knew she shouldn't be listening to a conversation that was none of her business. She made her face blank and feigned studying the back of a box of nasal decongestant.

Cameron leaned forward and spoke quietly to Bitsy. "He says you don't need it anymore."

Bitsy bristled. "I think I should be the one to decide if I need it anymore, don't you?" she asked, her voice sharp.

"I can't do anything, Bitsy. You'll have to talk to him." With a single nod, Cameron left the counter.

Bitsy stood without moving. She was still there when Cameron returned and called, "Mrs. Raymond?"

Lindy walked past Molly and went to the counter, and Molly soon caught up. Bitsy startled when she saw them.

"Hi, Bitsy," Molly said as Lindy handed her credit card to Cameron. She hoped Bitsy couldn't see in her face that she'd heard her conversation with the pharmacist. She said the first thing that popped into her mind. "Still on for the King's Heid?"

"Of course. I'm looking forward to it." Bitsy clearly forced a smile, then spun to leave. As she turned, her purse flew wide and knocked into a display of vitamins and supplements. The bag caught on the edge of the support for the display, and scores of little bottles went flying along with Bitsy's purse, its contents spilling everywhere.

When they hit the floor, the bottles clattered and rolled in every direction. Bitsy's phone went sailing and landed next to the sunglasses rack, and her collection of lipsticks and lip balms chased the vitamin bottles to hide in all available nooks and crannies. The lid on a plastic container of breath mints flew open and spit pink candies in a colorful shower. Tissues, a hairbrush, and a romance novel with a blush-inducing cover fell at Molly's feet.

Bitsy gave a little squawk and began chasing her belongings. Molly dropped to her knees and began picking up anything within reach. She grabbed truant vitamin bottles, putting them in an apron she made with her top. Sasha rushed out from behind the counter and crouched to help.

"How many bottles do you think there are?" Molly asked Sasha. "Fifty?"

"Eighty." Sasha's voice was clipped. "I know because I made the display."

When her top was full, Molly took her load to an empty spot on the pharmacy counter and deposited the bottles as gently as she could. As she righted each of the captured bottles, she was surprised when she pulled an empty prescription bottle with a childproof cap from her collection, then another with a couple of pills rattling around inside.

They hadn't been filled at MacPhee's because the labels were not only different from his but different from each other. She noted that Bitsy's name was on both bottles.

Bitsy's arm snaked past her and grabbed the two bottles. "Thanks. See you at dinner."

"Did you get all your lipstick, Bitsy?" Molly glanced down and saw a tube at her feet.

"No time. Lunch break." With a little wave, Bitsy disappeared down the aisle.

Five minutes later, Molly and Lindy had recovered every visible bottle and left Sasha to rebuild her display. Lindy sighed heavily as they started for the bakery. "I need a nap."

"Mmm," Molly replied.

Lindy eyed her. "What's wrong?"

"Pill bottles."

"I thought we got them all," Lindy said.

"Not those bottles." Molly's heart was heavy. "Bitsy's."

"She didn't pick up a prescription. The pharmacist told her the doctor wouldn't renew it."

"But she had two others. They fell out of her purse, and I picked them up."

"Three prescriptions if you count the one she can't get anymore." Lindy cringed. "Do you think she's really sick?"

Molly shook her head. "Three different prescriptions and three different pharmacies, two of which are at least half an hour away. That's the strange part. And the scary part." Molly angled to face Lindy. "If you have a perfectly good local pharmacy, why would you go out of town to get your medicine? And to two other pharmacies, not just one?"

Lindy raised an eyebrow. "Are you suggesting that she's doctor shopping? Or pharmacy shopping, I guess."

Molly winced at the term. "Maybe we've been hanging around Rick Capuana too much, but the only explanations I can come up with are troubling ones."

"Did you see what the prescriptions were for? Maybe she really is sick."

"Or maybe she's got a problem." Even saying it made Molly's stomach curdle.

"That's a pretty strong accusation without proof."

"I know." Molly glanced through the front window of Aff Yer Heid as they passed. A handful of women were having their hair cut and styled at the salon. "Maybe she had a procedure recently and was prescribed a strong painkiller."

"She's the elementary school principal. She can't have a problem. I mean, she can and maybe does, but what happens if anybody finds out?"

They walked in silence, thinking of the ramifications for Bitsy if people knew about her potential habit.

Molly drew in a breath as a thought leaped into her mind. "If we figured out what's up with Bitsy—"

"What we *think* is up with Bitsy," Lindy corrected. "I'm sensitive to the idea of false accusations at the moment."

"Right. As I was saying, if we figured it out, maybe Janae did too. Maybe Janae was holding it over Bitsy somehow."

"Blackmail!" Lindy scoffed. "Sounds just like Alana."

"It was one of the possibilities Rick mentioned when he was trying to figure out why she was at Crag Mallaig that night."

"It explains the man yelling *no more*."

"And Bitsy and the baseball bat."

"Alana was really asking for it, wasn't she?" Lindy grimaced. "Sorry, I shouldn't talk like that. It's not that killing her was right. Murder is always wrong."

"It is," Molly agreed, "but here's what I wonder. Why would Janae meet face to face with people? Why put herself in danger? These days, money can be transferred wirelessly and threats can be sent online. Why risk things going wrong by meeting in person?"

"I don't know. Maybe she was just old school."

"Maybe." Molly gestured toward the bakehouse as they approached the Victorian house. "Home sweet home."

"Thank goodness. I'm wiped out." Lindy headed for the exterior steps. "I need a nap."

"I bet you do."

"And I need some time to think about what Rick told me. I never thought I could feel grateful to him, but I do. Not knowing for sure what happened to Nate was eating at me." Lindy paused with her hand on the railing. "Now I have to decide whether to tell my mom. There are some things a mother shouldn't have to know."

16

Lindy went straight up to the apartment, but Molly stopped by the bakery kitchen and grabbed a couple of croissants. She brought them upstairs, split them, and filled them with chicken salad for a late lunch. She and Lindy ate in silence, both worn out from the morning.

While Lindy took a nap with Angus, Molly went to the bakery office to finish typing up the price list for the bakehouse's Guid Nychburris Day booth, which would be set up the next day. She, Carol, and Laura had decided to aim for a design that was cozy and warm rather than big-city sophistication. Loch Mallaig was a small town, and homey was their operative word.

Once she was happy with the price list and had proofread it twice, she printed it out on parchment-style paper and inserted it into a wooden document frame, then put it with the rest of the booth props.

Not sensing any sign of life from a still snoozing Lindy, Molly went down to check on the bakery and found Bridget rearranging the cases so the holes from all the day's sales weren't as obvious. It was nearly closing time, but they often got a rush at the end of the day, and Molly was glad to see Bridget taking the initiative to tidy up the displays.

With a jingle, the front door opened, and both Molly and Bridget turned to greet their newcomer.

"Hey, Dallis," Bridget said in greeting as the personal trainer smiled and approached the counter, an electronic tablet in his hands. "What can I get you?"

"Actually, I'm here to see Molly," he told Bridget.

"You have good timing," Molly said. "I just got here."

While Bridget continued tidying the cases, Dallis turned bright, eager eyes on Molly. "I did what you said."

Molly beamed. She knew what he was talking about. "You've made a video about your transformation? That's great."

"I've been working on it every spare moment," he said. "I got pictures from my sister and wrote a script, which I've never done before. I wanted to show you what I've done so far." He set his tablet on a table near the front window, tapped a few icons on the screen, and a video started to play, showing a photograph of Dallis as a little kid with big, blue eyes and lots of red curls.

"Cute." Molly had to grin.

He held up a finger. "Just wait."

Several pictures flashed, and in each he got older and more awkward until he was a plump teen with bad acne, braces, and slumped shoulders. Self-doubt cast a shadow over his entire demeanor. In a voice-over, Dallis spoke about his insecurities at the time, which were compounded by incessant bullying from other kids at school.

Dallis hit pause. "That's as far as I've gotten." He glanced at Molly. "What do you think?"

She gave him a quick hug. "It's wonderful. I'm so proud of you."

"It's not awful?"

"If that was the end, yes, it'd be pretty awful. But you've got the best yet to come."

Dallis took a deep breath. "You said that talking about secrets makes them lose their power."

"How wise of me," Molly joked.

"Any suggestions?" He indicated the tablet.

"Just one," Molly answered. "At the beginning, you need to introduce yourself. Some viewers will know who you are, but lots won't. That way your audience connects with you and wants to know your story."

Bridget cleared her throat. She'd approached them without Molly noticing. "Sorry to eavesdrop, but I took a video production class last semester. I can help you." She smiled at Dallis. "If you want."

"Really?" Dallis looked delighted. "I've been going online to watch tutorials on how to make professional-looking videos, but it's all Greek to me. Do you have any suggestions?"

Bridget opened her mouth as if she had something to say, then closed it.

"Don't be polite." Dallis pointed to the tablet. "Polite won't help me."

"Okay," Bridget said. "You'll want to incorporate graphics and music. We'll work up a cool treatment for *Dallis Witherspoon: From Bullied to Buff.*" She spread her hands as if she was spelling out the title card. "Your intro music plays over it. The same at the end with the extro playing over it."

"Extro?" Dallis raised an eyebrow.

"Exit music," Bridget explained. "You need someone to write you some original music. It'll be your theme music. No one else should have it but you."

The bakery door opened and Greer entered, taking a big, appreciative inhale and heading directly to the display cases. Bridget hurried back to her position behind the counter.

Dallis started to leave, but Molly laid a hand on his arm. "A quick question," she said quietly.

"Sure. What's up?"

"Did Janae threaten to blackmail you?"

Dallis's open expression darkened to wariness. "Why would you think that?"

"You asked me on Tuesday if I'd think badly of you if pictures of you as an awkward kid hit the Internet," Molly reminded him. "I asked if you'd been threatened with their release, and you never answered. Since then, I've learned several things about Janae. I wouldn't be surprised if she threatened you."

The trainer's gaze darted around the room, landing everywhere but on Molly.

She decided to say what she was thinking. "You were there Tuesday night, weren't you?"

He took a step backward. "I never hurt her."

Molly shook her head. She knew Dallis. "Of course you didn't. But did you want to scare her? Is that why you brought the gun?"

"What gun?" He sounded genuinely startled by the question. "I don't have a gun. And I certainly wouldn't bring it with me on a late-night jog."

Molly was confused. "One of the witnesses that night heard a gunshot."

Dallis frowned, then his expression cleared. "I couldn't sleep so I went for a run, and I came across Janae in the park. She started taunting me about the photos she had, and I guess it brought back memories of those high school bullies. I closed my eyes to try to block her out, but she kicked a trash can by the crag to get my attention. That was the noise, not a gunshot."

Molly nodded. The noise of a trash can being kicked could easily sound like a gunshot to already frightened kids.

He suddenly seemed to realize what she'd said and narrowed his eyes at her. "Wait, what witnesses are you talking about?"

"There were four kids on the other side of the crag, and they heard your conversation with Janae."

"There were kids there?" Dallis's face paled behind his tan. "And the police know I was there?"

"The police are aware there was a man present, but not who as far as I know." Molly glanced at Greer, who was paying for her bag of pastries, then settled her gaze back on Dallis. "Maybe it's time they find out."

Before Dallis could respond, Greer approached them, a smile on her face. "Dallis, you don't know what you're missing," she said, apparently aware of Dallis's notorious willpower. She opened her bag and waved it under his nose, clearly enjoying goading him. "Have you ever had a melting moment?"

Dallis feigned a look of horror and held up a hand. "Get thee behind me, Satan."

"Your loss, big guy." Greer pulled a shortbread sandwich cookie from her bag and made a production of taking a bite. "Mmmmmm!"

Dallis shuddered and grabbed his tablet. "Bridget, I'll call to set up a time to meet." He hesitated. "Greer, I'll walk you out."

Molly locked the door behind them, hoping that Dallis would have the courage to tell Greer he'd been in Dumfries Park on Tuesday night. If he didn't, she thought with a guilty shiver, she might have to do it for him.

A short time later, Bridget, Carol, and Laura had gone home, and the bakehouse went dark for the day. Molly collected Angus from the apartment, still seeing no sign that Lindy had awoken from her nap.

"Come on, boy," she told her eager Scottie as she snapped on his leash. "Let's go for a walk by the lake."

They strolled through the park, then crossed Yooper Boulevard and got onto the lakeside walking path that followed the road. A family was having a picnic at a table near the pier, but otherwise Molly and Angus were alone. Loch Mallaig was peaceful as a mirror, the water a sheet of blue satin without wrinkle or blemish. The quiet felt like a healing balm on Molly's nerves, frazzled by the mysteries churning in her mind.

A pair of merganser ducks cruised by, a brood of seven ducklings trailing them. Farther out on the water, a loon floated with a chick sitting comfortably on her back. An osprey soared overhead, searching the lake for his dinner.

When Molly and Angus reached the spot where Loch Ness Lane intersected Yooper Boulevard, they took the crosswalk so they could go back to Bread on Arrival through the park.

"Bang! Bang! Pow! Pow!" Youthful shouting tore through the calm.

"So much for quiet," Molly muttered as she and Angus glanced around to find the source of the sound. Ahead, a boy was climbing on Crag Mallaig, pretending to shoot all his imaginary enemies with abandon.

Even from this distance, Molly recognized Robby MacDuff.

Molly slowed their pace and watched Robby for a little while. Somehow seeing him playing like any boy might—climbing rocks, playing good guys versus bad guys—made her feel better about him. He wasn't just a sly kid who was too full of himself. He was also a regular boy with a regular imagination.

He climbed up the crag until he stood on the highest point. He raised his arms in victory, undoubtedly hearing the applause of the crowd at his amazing feat.

Angus gave a little woof that Molly feared was the prelude to a loud barking riff.

"Shush," she said gently. "We don't want to embarrass him. He's having too much fun."

Angus complied, and Molly watched as Robby lowered his arms and got down on his knees. Even with several yards between them, Molly could tell his body language had changed. Instead of a kid having fun, he'd gone serious. He reached out and down, stretching his arm and upper body as far as they would go. For a moment, she thought he was going to tumble head first, but he scrambled back just before he tipped over. He stood again, and he pulled something up with him.

A bat.

He gripped it like a ballplayer might, and from his position on top of the crag, feigned hitting a game-winning home run.

Molly froze. A bat!

"Robby!" She began running. "No! Don't!"

Robby spun at her voice and lost his footing. The bat went flying end over end as he teetered. He fell to his knees and grabbed hold of the rock. As she neared, she could see his shocked and frightened face.

He held on as his feet fought for traction. Finally, one toe found a little ledge and he stabilized.

"Are you okay?" she called.

"You scared me!" He pulled himself back to the top of the crag and glared down at her. His fierce anger vibrated in the air. She noticed his left knee was scraped, and he was shaking his hands as if his fingers hurt.

"Can you get down?" she asked. "Do you need help?"

He stared at her as if the very suggestion that he needed help from anyone, let alone her, was the most ludicrous thing he'd ever heard. With one last get-lost glare at Molly, he started to climb down. "Where's that . . ."

He wanted the bat.

Not if she could help it. She ran in the direction she'd seen it fly. She had to beat him to it. She spotted it on the far side of the crag, wedged between two rocks.

She reached the bat before Robby. Knowing he considered it his by right of discovery, she did something she doubted Chief Thomson would approve of. She snatched it up.

She knew she held the murder weapon.

"Hey! That's mine!" Robby reached for the bat, ready to grab it from her hands.

She stuck it behind her back. "Sorry, Robby. It's evidence."

"I found it. It's mine."

"Doesn't matter." Molly shook her head. "It's not yours."

"It's . . . it's Ms. Barkley's." Robby's eyes lit up with pride at his own cleverness. "I-I was going to give it back to her."

"No, Robby. We need to give it to the police."

Knowledge widened his eyes. He stared at the bat. "That's what Ms. Barkley used on Mrs. Harbison?" He stepped back, and his brow creased with worry. "You're going to tell them why my fingerprints are on it, right?"

"I'll tell them, but everyone knows you didn't have anything to do with the murder, Robby. You were always with your friends."

"Right. I was." He relaxed for a moment, then tensed again. "Until they left me." The betrayal clearly still rankled.

"But then you were with me."

"Oh yeah." He brightened.

Holding the bat carefully with two fingers slotted just under the knob, Molly pulled out her phone and dialed the police station. When Wilma Guthrie answered, Molly braced herself for a long conversation with the gossip-mongering receptionist. Fortunately, Wilma must have been distracted by another matter because she put Molly through to Chief Thomson without comment.

While she waited for him to pick up, Molly examined the bat carefully. The letters *LMES* were written in black permanent marker on the knob, which had a good-sized chip out of it so the S was only half a snake. Loch Mallaig Elementary School, at a guess. The cap of the bat was stained dark brown. She glanced away quickly, feeling her stomach roll.

Knowing that Robby had tainted the bat with his retrieval of it and his mighty swing, she wondered how much helpful evidence remained for the state lab to find.

Molly was startled from her ruminations by the chief coming on the line. "This is Chief Thomson."

After identifying herself, Molly quickly said, "Please come to Crag Mallaig right away. I've found something you need to see. Or I should say, Robby MacDuff found something you need to see."

In no time, Crag Mallaig was once again teeming with police. Officer Murdoch donned latex gloves and carefully collected the bat from Molly before slipping it into an oversize evidence bag. Chief Thomson dispatched Greer to personally drive the bat to the state lab for forensics work. "We need this done yesterday. Tell them that."

The officer took the carefully bagged bat and left.

"You found this up there?" Chief Thomson asked Robby as he pointed up the crag.

Robby, apparently enjoying his role in this drama, nodded. "I was just climbing, you know. I reached the top and looked down. There it was, stuck in a little opening." He held his hands close together. "The letters on the end caught my attention."

"They weren't very big," the chief said.

Robby shrugged. "No, but they didn't belong, you know?"

"Can you show us where you found it?"

"Sure." The boy frowned at the chief uncertainly. "Are you going to climb up with me?"

"Not me," the chief said with a laugh. "Officer Murdoch will go."

The young officer raised an eyebrow at the rocks. "Me?"

"Since you missed an important piece of evidence last time, yes, you." The chief gestured. "Follow the boy."

Molly had to swallow a laugh as Robby took off with the sure-footedness of a mountain goat and Dalziel followed with considerably less enthusiasm.

"Make sure to take lots of pictures, Dalziel," Chief Thomson called.

With a nod of acknowledgment, Dalziel continued his awkward climb.

"What's going on?" Lindy appeared at Molly's side. "I woke up and peeked out the window, and all I saw were police cars and flashing lights. Was someone else hurt?"

Molly shook her head. "We found the bat."

Lindy's eyes widened. "*The* bat?"

"The very one."

Lindy gripped Molly's elbow, her eyes bright with interest. "Tell me everything."

17

"Nice to see you again, Mrs. Ferris." The raven-haired hostess at the King's Heid Pub smiled as Molly and Lindy entered the restaurant.

"You too, Kirsty." *Apparently I come here more often than I realized,* Molly thought, though she figured that her friendship with Fergus—and the fact that they often dined together after the occasional golf lessons he gave her—had something to do with her familiarity with the hostess. The knowing smirks worn by Carol and Laura, who were seated on a bench in the foyer, indicated that they thought the same thing.

"Sorry we're late," Molly told her friends. She and Lindy had had to scramble to get ready and arrive on time after the latest excitement in the park.

"It's only a few minutes past six," Laura said. "Besides, Bitsy isn't here yet anyway."

"Would you like me to seat you?" the hostess asked. "Or would you like to wait for the rest of your party?"

Molly wasn't entirely sure whether or not Bitsy would show after the pill bottle fiasco. She was wondering how to answer the hostess when Bitsy bustled into the restaurant, appearing quite frazzled.

"I am so sorry," Bitsy told the women a bit breathlessly. "Miss Priss ate something that made her sick and I had to take her to the vet. She's got to spend the night."

"Oh no." Lindy gave Bitsy a hug. "That poor baby."

"Is she going to be all right?" Molly knew the cat was Bitsy's family, and her illness would be one more stress added to the many already pressing in.

"They said tonight was just for observation, so I think she'll be fine." Bitsy didn't sound as though she believed her own words entirely. "I should be able to get her tomorrow."

"Then you need dinner with friends to take your mind off the trauma." Lindy patted Bitsy's arm.

"Ready?" Kirsty asked, a stack of leather-bound menus in her hands. "Mr. MacGregor had me set aside our best table for you." She led them across the dining room to their table, which gave them a beautiful view of the golf course in the golden light of evening. Once Molly and her friends were seated, Kirsty handed out menus, mentioned the specials, then told them the name of their server and gracefully disappeared.

After remarking on the spectacular view, everyone began to study the menu. They oohed and aahed over the tempting selections, and eventually made up their minds—chicken pot pie for Molly, steak and potatoes au gratin for Laura, grilled salmon and risotto for Lindy and Carol, and shrimp scampi for Bitsy. They gave their orders to their server, a handsome, charming college kid working at Castleglen for the summer.

Dinner passed with good food and much laughter as the women shared stories from their professional pasts. The finely chopped vegetables in the salad course inspired Laura to tell the others about the head chef at the New York restaurant where she'd worked before 29 North. "He had this big knife that he never put down. It was like an extension of his arm, and he talked with his hands a lot." She demonstrated with slashing motions. "The line chefs lived in mortal fear every day. I'm pretty sure I extended my life by years when I moved to 29 North."

"I never feared for my life as a math teacher, thank goodness." Carol chuckled. "The closest I ever got to a dangerous situation was the time the electricity went out in the cafeteria. It was an inside room with no windows. Pandemonium ensued, as you can imagine. When the lights finally came back on, though, all the desserts had disappeared."

"Never question the power of sugar," Molly said with a laugh. "I think it goes to show we're in the right business. Maybe we should be marketing to a younger crowd more often."

"They certainly shouldn't be underestimated," Bitsy said as she skewered a shrimp on her fork.

Laura smiled. "You must have a million stories, Bitsy."

"I have my fair share," Bitsy agreed. "One that really sticks in my mind was a few years ago. A young entrepreneur at Loch Mallaig Elementary told all his classmates that a famous singer was coming to perform in the school gym, and tickets were only $10 each. The kid collected a bundle before one of the mothers asked me if the singer was really coming. When I asked the boy how he planned to deal with all his irate classmates when the star didn't show, he said he was going to tell them the singer had a sore throat and couldn't come. He expected everyone would simply be okay with that and he'd get to keep all their money."

Everyone laughed heartily, then Lindy shook her head. "Unfortunately, sometimes adults are the ones acting like children." She elbowed Molly. "Remember the wedding reception that erupted into a food fight?"

"I'll never forget." Molly shook her head. "Talk about tension. It was the Montagues and Capulets come to life. The bride's family didn't like the groom's family, and the feeling was mutual with a vengeance. In fact, the only two who seemed at all happy were the bride and groom."

Lindy took up the story. "The groom's brother got upset at a crack the bride's brother made about the groom. He poured a glass of champagne on the brother's head. The brother grabbed a fistful of the mashed potatoes on his dinner plate and threw it at the best man, and the fight was on."

Molly cringed at the memory. "When it was finished, the bride stood in the middle of the dance floor with tears streaming down her face, multiple foods running down her dress, and wedding cake in her hair. Her veil had disappeared somewhere in the melee. The groom was laid out flat at her feet because he'd stepped on some gravy in his slippery dress shoes, went flying, and hit his head. He was out cold for most of it."

"By the time he woke up, the police had detained half the guests," Lindy added.

"And I thought event planning was a classy job," Carol said. "How did you two keep from getting plastered with food? Or didn't you?"

Lindy and Molly glanced at each other and laughed. Molly answered Carol's question. "As soon as the champagne was poured on the brother's head, we escaped into the hallway. We might arrange an event, but we wanted no part in disarranging it."

Lindy held up a finger. "Last I heard, the bride and groom moved to Alaska and haven't communicated with their families in three years."

"That's better than the ending of *Romeo and Juliet*," Laura said.

They were all still laughing when their server returned and asked if they wanted to order dessert. Everyone looked at Laura since she and Fergus's son, Neil, worked together on what cakes, pies, and other sweets Bread on Arrival provided for the King's Heid.

"A slice each of the dark chocolate cake and the lemon chiffon pie, and five dessert forks," Laura told the waiter.

Laura's selections were spot-on, and Molly felt aglow with happiness after they'd wrapped up their meal and headed for the exit. Lindy excused herself to the restroom on the way out, telling Molly she'd meet her at her car.

Laura and Carol got to their vehicles first and drove off with waves. Since Molly and Bitsy had arrived a few minutes later, their cars were farther back in the lot. They walked together to Bitsy's MINI Cooper.

"That was such a nice night." Bitsy pulled out her keys and hit the unlock fob. The click was audible in the quiet parking lot. "I needed to relax a bit."

"I'll bet," Molly said, then took a deep breath. Bitsy's relaxation was about to come to an end. "There's no easy way to bring this up, but I figure you should know—the bat has been found."

Bitsy froze. Her voice shaking slightly, she finally squeaked, "What bat?"

"The bat that was used to kill Janae."

Bitsy's keys fell to the ground, but she didn't retrieve them. "A bat was used to kill Janae?" she whispered.

"Not just *a* bat, Bitsy. The bat that you brought to Crag Mallaig Tuesday night was the murder weapon."

Bitsy blinked at Molly, her eyes huge and haunted. "You believe I brought a bat to Crag Mallaig Tuesday night? Why would you even think I was there?" She tried to laugh but the sound was strangled.

"Robby, Cara, Ian, and Maggie saw you arrive at Crag Mallaig with the bat in your hand."

Bitsy shook her head. "If I was there, why would I help you track them down to question them? They must be mistaken."

Molly smiled sadly. "We both know they're not."

"But . . ." She studied Molly's knowing expression. Then she sagged against the car, broken. "I never used it. I swear!"

"No?" Molly let her skepticism show. "Then how did it get to the top of Crag Mallaig?"

"I swung it. I even banged it against the rocks. I wanted to scare her and get her to leave me alone. I was caught up in the moment.

When I realized what I was doing, I tossed it aside and ran. I think it rolled up against a tree trunk, but I don't know for sure."

"You didn't throw it upward? It was found in a crevice near the top of Crag Mallaig."

Bitsy shook her head, her red curls bouncing with the denial. "I never could throw very well, even as a kid."

Molly studied Bitsy. If she hadn't thrown the bat, then who had?

"Who found it?" Bitsy asked.

"Robby MacDuff. He was climbing on the rocks and discovered it by accident."

"And you know all this how?" Bitsy asked, desperation in her voice.

"Angus and I were taking a walk and saw Robby find it. I called the police."

"Do the police know I brought a bat with me that night?" Bitsy's face had taken on a gray cast.

"They do. The kids told them. They might have traced it to you anyway since the bat has *LMES* on the knob. Loch Mallaig Elementary School."

"It had a broken knob, and I was afraid some child would get a splinter." Bitsy sounded defeated. "I had the bat in my office with the idea of replacing it. When I knew I was going to meet Janae, I took it with me. But only to use as a threat."

"She was blackmailing you, wasn't she?" Molly ventured.

"Blackmailing me?" Bitsy repeated. "You must be kidding."

"Come on, Bitsy. She knew about the pills, didn't she?"

Bitsy closed her eyes and dropped her head. "She was messing with my whole life."

"She tried it with me when I first moved here too."

"She did?" Bitsy's head snapped up in astonishment.

Anger still simmered as Molly remembered that conversation.

"The difference between me and you is that I really had nothing she could twist to her advantage."

Bitsy sighed a long, ragged breath. "I had rotator cuff surgery at Christmas break. At the end of February, Janae approached me one night after Leaping Lowlanders. 'How's the pain? I bet it's still bothering you.' Without a second thought I told her it was. I told her how the physical therapy hurt, and my job required me to feel good even when I didn't. 'I know a guy,' she said, 'a doctor who will keep you supplied with what you need.' I'm ashamed that *need* had become the operative word."

"Janae really knew how to kick you when you were down."

"It was so easy to say yes to her, but then she turned on me." The misery on Bitsy's face was as much self-loathing as defeat. "How could this happen to me? I'm a responsible person. I have an important job. If the community ever found out that I have a problem, I'd be unemployed by the next board of education meeting."

Molly was gratified to hear Bitsy's admission. "So consider all this a wake-up call. How do you plan to take advantage of it?"

Bitsy's shoulders lifted in a hopeless shrug. "I don't know. I'm scared. I need the medicine."

"Stop thinking in terms of medicine, Bitsy. You don't need medicine. You need help."

Bitsy brushed at a tear that slid down her cheek. "I need help," she whispered. "But if anyone learns I'm in treatment . . ."

"Better they learn you're dealing with the problem than they learn you've kept using," Molly said firmly.

Bitsy let out a puff of air. "It sounds so reasonable when you say it, but I'm scared to death."

"It all starts with acknowledging the truth."

Bitsy hugged herself as if she was standing coatless in January rather than on a warm night in June.

Molly bent and picked up Bitsy's fallen keys. "School must be over for the summer any day now."

Bitsy nodded. "Tomorrow."

"Summer would be a good time to go away for a while and get the help you need. I'll even watch Miss Priss for you if you're worried about her."

"I'll think about it." Bitsy took her keys and climbed in her car.

Molly watched her drive off with a hesitant heart. Would she really consider getting treatment? Or would she cause herself more pain by ignoring the problem?

18

Bread on Arrival's front door bell jingled just as Molly was busing plates and coffee cups from the café area. She smiled at Fergus and Harvey as they entered. "You're right on time," she said.

"My wife raised me right," Harvey joked. "I'm a retired writer, not exactly a recipe for punctuality. If it weren't for Carol, I'd be three days late to everything."

Molly chuckled. She knew that was far from true for the dependable Harvey, but she appreciated the clear affection he had for Carol. "Well I'm glad she's rubbed off on you."

"I'm only here for the cookies." Fergus smiled, his light blue eyes twinkling.

"As many as you can eat," Molly promised, then grinned. "After you're done setting up our Guid Nychburris Day booth."

"Lead the way," Harvey said, then followed Molly as she took them into the kitchen. When they passed a rack filled with trays of cooling shortbread, Harvey sniffed appreciatively.

"Don't even think about it," Carol warned from across the room, where she was frosting cupcakes. "Those are for the booth." Then her sternness vanished and she winked. "I saved a dozen of the chocolate-dipped ones. I know they're your favorite."

"You're too good to me," Harvey said, clutching his heart. "Now I'd better go earn them."

Molly showed the men to the storage room where they kept several eight-foot folding tables. Fergus stopped right beside her, and she could smell the clean, woodsy scent of his soap. Her heart gave a little leap, which she tried to ignore.

Harvey grabbed hold of a table and started to slide it out. "This isn't too heavy," he told Fergus. "I'll get this one, you get the next one." He grasped the handle and hauled the table out of the room toward the back door, which Laura had propped open.

"Are the tables all you've got?" Fergus asked as he grabbed the end of the next table in the stack.

At his tone of voice, Molly felt a stab of uncertainty, then shook it off and tapped into her confidence as a veteran event planner. "I have a framed menu and some brochures about the mail-order service we're launching. I have napkins with a thistle design, and Bridget is arranging some wildflower bouquets. We'll cover the tables with plaid blankets, but I'm not doing that until tomorrow because I don't want them getting damp overnight. The food will be showcased on shiny metal trays to attract attention. It'll look very pretty when I'm finished."

"Sounds great." Fergus nodded approval. "How many tables do you need?"

"Four. Two at the front of the booth and two at the back for storage and supplies." Curiosity—not a desire to extend the conversation as long as possible, she told herself—made her ask, "How many tables does the Castleglen booth usually have?"

"Only one, usually, but we typically just put out brochures and branded pens." Fergus grinned. "Although Neil is in charge this year, and he's got some creative plans, like raffles for a free round of golf and a spa package."

"Clever ideas," Molly said. "It's not much out of your pocket, and it's wonderful exposure for the resort."

"I'm glad the PR guru approves." He leaned the table he'd been pulling against the door jamb. He suddenly seemed unsure. "There's something else I'd like your approval on."

"What is it?"

Fergus hoisted the table and nodded toward the door. "Come with me."

With a smile at Harvey as he passed them on his way to getting another table from the storage room, Molly followed Fergus out the back door to his Range Rover, which he'd parked beside the bakery. Harvey's table was already in the back, alongside a large white bundle that Molly recognized immediately. "Thank you again for loaning us a tent. You'll have to let me know what the rental fee is."

"You get the friends and family discount, so you don't owe me anything. You don't want your goodies—or yourselves—to be in the sun all day," Fergus said, visibly pleased at Molly's gratitude. "We have tons of tents at the resort. We won't miss one for the weekend."

"Thank you, Fergus," she repeated, touched by his generosity.

"That's not all." He reached into the car and brought out a roll of white vinyl nestled next to the tent. "I took a liberty with this, but I hope you'll like it."

He unrolled the fabric to reveal a beautiful banner with the bakehouse's name on it in a Celtic font. Molly couldn't keep herself from clapping at the sight of it. It was the perfect finishing touch for the booth.

"We were having a new banner printed for the resort's booth," Fergus explained. "I had them print one similar to your grand opening banner, but with just the business name so you can use it whenever you need to."

"It's perfect!" Molly hugged him, and he returned her embrace with one hand since the other still had the banner in it. "I was going to try and use the grand opening one, but this is even better."

"I'm glad you like it," he said when she stepped away to look at the banner again. "We'll mount it on the tent so people can see it from far away."

Harvey arrived with another table, which he set on the ground so he could pat Fergus on the back. "Way to impress the girl. I told you it would work."

Molly blushed at Harvey's comment. Was a slight flush coloring Fergus's cheeks too?

Fergus cleared his throat. "What's your booth number, Molly? Harvey and I will have you set up in no time."

"We're 19," Molly said. "I'd be happy to come help if you want."

"I'm sure we can handle the basics, and then you can make it pretty tomorrow," Fergus said. "You've got a great location in the middle of the food area. People will buy meat pasties at the Neeps and Tatties booth, then come over to Bread on Arrival for dessert."

"I sure hope so," Molly said.

A short while later, Fergus and Harvey set out with the tables, tent, and banner as well as a bakery box of shortbread each. After waving goodbye, Molly returned to the kitchen. "We've got a tent and a banner," she announced to Laura and Carol. "We're going to look like we know what we're doing, thanks to Fergus."

"I think we were already going to look like we know what we're doing thanks to you," Carol said, "but I'm glad he helped."

"I can't wait to see it all put together," Laura said as she pulled fresh loaves of fragrant oat bread from the oven. "Though I'm not sure when. I'm hoping Hamish, Carol, and I stay extra-busy here too. We're close to the park, so fingers crossed we get lots of traffic from festival goers who want to get out of the sun for a bit."

"I'm sure you can sneak away at some point," Molly said. "Even if it's just to deliver more bread and cookies to me and Bridget at the booth."

"And me too," Lindy said as she entered the kitchen. "I'll pitch in at the booth."

"Your family's coming," Molly said. "You need to be with them."

"Yes, when they get here," Lindy replied. "It's a six-hour drive, remember? I'll have the whole morning to help."

Molly was glad to see her friend feeling energetic again after the previous day's asthma scare. "Then we'd love to have you at the booth."

Lindy grinned. "Working together like old times."

"You should see what Fergus has for us." Molly beamed. "He and Harvey are setting up our booth right now."

"Let's go check it out," Lindy suggested.

"Go." Laura made a shooing motion with her oven mitts. "This is your semi-vacation, remember?"

Molly headed for the door right behind Lindy. "I owe you."

Laura laughed. "Don't worry. We'll collect."

"You can count on that," Carol agreed.

Giggling like a couple of kids whose mother had excused them from cleaning their rooms, Molly and Lindy crossed the backyard. Just beyond the gate, they entered a hive of pre-festival activity. Organized chaos stood before them, with dozens of people buzzing around booths in varying stages of setup. A man putting up a display of water sports equipment sang at the top of his lungs with the country music playing over the loudspeaker. A kind woman from the chamber of commerce was offering cups of coffee to anyone who passed her table. A clever teen walked around with a rolling cooler selling bottled water.

Lindy flicked a hand in the direction of the singer. "Someone should tell him silence is golden."

Molly grinned. "But he's having so much fun."

They wandered down to the pier, where a temporary stage was being built—the stage where Molly would perform with the rest of The

Leaping Lowlanders. The thought of actually dancing up there where people could see her made Molly's stomach twist in protest, and not only because of pre-performance jitters. That stage didn't look quite large enough to handle all the dancers, especially with them moving around so much.

A truck backed to the stage area, and the driver began unloading microphones, speakers, and a sound board. Molly watched with growing relief as he began to snap a portable dance floor together on the ground in front of the stage. That would give The Leaping Lowlanders plenty of space.

Molly and Lindy continued their walk through the festival grounds and eventually found booth 19, where Fergus and Harvey had just finished putting up Bread on Arrival's tent.

"Looking good," Molly said in greeting. "How can we help?"

Fergus shook his head. "We've got it. Come back in about half an hour, and you can tell us if the banner is hung right."

Molly felt a rush of gratitude for Fergus's foresight. "Anything you do with the banner will be fine by me."

"Remember you said that." With a cheery wave, he started back to his Range Rover to get a table.

"Where to next?" Lindy asked Molly, glancing around.

"Good question," Molly answered, also scanning their surroundings. She paused when her gaze landed on Crag Mallaig, which lay several yards beyond where the festival preparation ended. Even from this distance, she recognized a uniformed Greer Anderson climbing the rocks. "And there's the answer."

Lindy frowned in confusion. "What's she up to?"

"Let's go find out."

A few minutes later, they reached Crag Mallaig. Catching sight of her new audience, Greer waved in acknowledgment.

"Careful up there," Molly called, remembering how Robby had nearly fallen.

"Don't worry about me." Greer chuckled. "My mom always said I was half mountain goat."

Making the ascent look easy, Greer reached the top of the crag, where she balanced confidently on the uneven surface. She pulled out her phone and studied a picture. She scanned the area, then pointed. "There's the crevice."

For a few minutes, Molly and Lindy waited quietly while Greer apparently assessed the rocks. Perhaps she was trying to determine which side of Crag Mallaig the bat had been tossed from. But would that help her track down a killer? Molly certainly hoped so. Eventually, Greer finished her examination and edged away from the crevice.

"Find what you were looking for?" Molly asked.

Greer started her descent. "I'm glad you're here," she said instead of answering. "I wanted to talk to you."

"Does she mean you or me?" Lindy murmured to Molly.

"Both of you," Greer answered.

"Relax," Molly urged Lindy. "She doesn't think I'm guilty, so she doesn't think you're guilty either."

"Guilty of what?" Greer called.

"In addition to being half goat, you may also be part bat," Molly said. "You've got good ears."

"I do," Greer agreed. "Guilty of what?"

"Killing Janae." Molly shook her head. "Lindy thinks she's a suspect."

"Well." Greer jumped the final few feet to the ground. "You've got motive, don't you, Lindy?"

"I suppose so." Lindy shot a smirk at Molly. "See? I told you."

Greer waved a hand through the air. "I can tell you that your prints aren't on the bat, and we know beyond any doubt that the bat was the murder weapon."

"The dark stain?" Molly swallowed bile.

Greer nodded, sending her blonde ponytail swinging. "The lab reports came in this morning."

"Were there any usable prints, or had Robby and I messed them up too much?" Molly asked.

"It was full of fingerprints." Greer crossed her arms. "Most of them belonging to kids since apparently Bitsy Barkley borrowed it from her school. But no kid killed Janae Harbison."

"Certainly not," Molly said, aghast at the idea.

"However, there were also two sets of adult prints." Greer arched an eyebrow at Molly. "Besides yours that is."

"I know one is Bitsy's," Molly said. "Whose was the other?"

Greer laughed. "I can't reveal that. The chief would kill me."

"So you know who the second person is?" Molly paused as a few puzzle pieces clicked together. "That means the prints are on file, and he or she has a record."

"Which brings me to my question for you," Greer said, not responding to Molly's comment. "You have all kinds of people coming into Bread on Arrival, especially this week with the festival. Do you recognize the name Wanda Joy Kowalski?"

Molly shook her head. "Doesn't ring a bell. Is she the second—"

Greer held up a hand. "Don't even try it. I have shared way too much already."

"Can you tell me what she looks like?"

"Even if I could, I can't. I don't know. There was a glitch in the database and her photo didn't come through." With a shrug and a wave, Greer strolled toward the path that would lead her out of the park. "See you ladies later."

Molly stared after the officer, confused by her nonchalance. "How can she be so cavalier?"

Lindy splayed her hands wide. "She's well practiced at being patient. In her job, it doesn't pay to waste energy on things you can't control."

"True." Still, Molly groaned. "I'm not that patient."

Lindy laughed at her. "Poor uninformed Molly. All you have to do is figure out who Wanda Joy is."

Molly groaned again, thinking about all the visitors in town for Guid Nychburris Day. Wanda Jean Kowalski could be any of them. "Simple as that, huh?" Molly shook her head. If there was one thing she was certain of, nothing about Janae Harbison's life—or death—was simple.

19

"Are you ready?" Molly called from her bedroom later that morning. "Time to go."

"Ready." Lindy joined her in the upstairs hall. "How do I look?"

Molly inspected her friend. "Not bad for someone who didn't know she'd be going to a funeral when she packed."

"Thanks for loaning me a dark blouse to go with my black slacks." Lindy glanced down at herself. "I may look okay, but my stomach is jumping with nerves."

Molly reached for the door. "You'll be fine. I know how important it is to you to make sure Skye is doing okay."

Lindy fidgeted, but nodded agreement. "I didn't expect to be this nervous."

Molly gave a reassuring smile. "Remember, Skye doesn't know who you are. No reason to panic about spending time in the same room with her."

"Easy for you to say."

Molly shrugged. "True."

The tap of toenails on hardwood sounded as Angus danced to the door.

"Oh, buddy, I'm sorry," Molly said sympathetically. "You can't come with us this time."

The little Scottie sat and pouted at her with the saddest eyes.

Molly was unmoved. "You would not enjoy a funeral. You'd have to sit still for a long time, and we both know you can't be still unless you're sleeping. And if you're sleeping, you might as well be comfortable here at home on your bed."

Angus gave a snort. Was it from dust or disgust?

Molly bent and gave him a pet goodbye.

Seeming to accept his fate, he walked into the bedroom. As she collected her purse and keys, she heard him jump onto her bed.

A short while later, Molly pulled her car into a spot at Fitzgerald Funeral Home, then she and Lindy entered the solemn silence of the vestibule. A younger man in a black suit gave them a small program and indicated with the wave of his arm where they should go. Judging by his age, Molly figured he was likely a friend of Skye's who had volunteered to serve as an usher.

She and Lindy took their places in the back of the short receiving line at the door of the chapel. A pair of women in their early thirties stood in front of them, and Molly wondered if they were a couple of the young moms who had exited Dancing on Air with their kids the day she and Lindy had been outside.

At the front of the line were a couple of high school girls. They hugged Skye, who was dressed in a dark green dress that flattered her coloring and lithe dancer's figure. The poor girl probably didn't own a black dress appropriate for a funeral. Why would she?

Next, the girls said hello to Verna, who was on the far side of Skye, wearing all black right down to the circles under her eyes. Instead of paying respects at the coffin after greeting Verna, the girls joined a large group of teens that filled the back rows of chairs.

This is probably their first funeral, Molly mused. *I don't blame them for not wanting to stop by the coffin.* As she watched the teens, Molly could tell that they were doing their best to be respectful in this uncomfortable situation, though she did hear the occasional giggle escape their hushed conversation.

A few moments later, Molly was in front of Skye, who shook her hand politely with a vague sense of recognition. Molly's appearance at a few Leaping Lowlander rehearsals probably hadn't left much of an imprint on the girl.

"I'm so sorry, Skye." Molly had learned when Kevin died that those simple words sincerely spoken were the best ones for this worst of times.

"Thank you for coming." The girl's voice was gracious but distant.

"Verna." Molly moved along and took the woman's hand in both of hers. "I'm so sorry."

"Thanks so much for coming, Molly," Verna said, her voice raspy. "It was kind of you."

"This whole thing has got to be a nightmare for both you and Skye."

Verna glanced at the girl, who was smiling politely but with zero recognition at Lindy. "She's such a good kid. She doesn't deserve any of this."

Lindy moved up behind Molly and whispered, "This is hard. I've got to sit down."

"Are you okay?" Molly asked, concerned.

Lindy gave a little shrug and moved past Molly and Verna to the third row.

A giggle broke into the quiet, and Skye and two girlfriends who had just approached her put their hands to their mouths. They glanced around guiltily, and tried to act restrained.

"I'm glad she can laugh," Verna said to Molly. "Last week, she took her last high school finals. This week . . ." She indicated the funeral home. "Poor kid."

Molly squeezed Verna's hands again. "Let me know if there's anything I can do to help."

Verna peered at her closely. "Do you mean that?"

Molly blinked. "Of course."

"Would you be willing to go to my house after we're finished here and make certain things are in order for any guests that come? I did some cleaning, but I might have missed something with everything that's been going on. Mr. Fitzgerald will tell people they're invited for refreshments and fellowship, and Skye has been inviting her friends as if it was a party."

"We'll be glad to help." Molly thought Lindy would be excited about the chance to spend more time with Skye. "What do you want me to do?"

"I ordered some food trays from The Hamper, but I'm worried we won't be home before the delivery arrives," Verna said. "Could you go accept the delivery and make sure everything looks okay? I don't want Skye to be embarrassed."

"Sure." Molly smiled. "Don't worry about a thing."

Verna got her purse from a chair in the front row of chairs. Aside from the high school kids in the back, very few of the other seats were filled. "Here's the house key." She thrust a key chain at Molly.

Molly accepted the key, then sat down beside Lindy. "We're going to their house to help after the service. And stop staring at Skye."

"Am I staring?" Lindy blinked in surprise. "I didn't realize. I'll stop—or at least try to. And helping how?"

"Going to the house to make sure things are ready for visitors."

"Really?" Lindy's face brightened, then she caught herself. She tried to look somber, but she couldn't entirely bury her grin.

The service was short, less than ten minutes long. A local pastor quoted a few well-known Bible verses, but it was clear he didn't know Janae. No one stood to give a eulogy, not even Skye or Verna.

As Oliver Fitzgerald gave instructions to those going to the cemetery, Molly thought about how different her own husband's funeral had been. Kevin's service had lasted more than an hour, as person after person shared how much he'd meant to them. Their minister had told stories about Kevin as someone who knew him well. They'd sung songs and hymns Kevin had loved, the singing led by one of Kevin's golfing buddies. Everything was personal and full of love. Most importantly, Chloe was so proud of her father to this day, based in part on what everyone had said about him then.

What did Skye have to remember?

Molly unlocked the front door of Verna's and Skye's house. She and Lindy walked down a hallway into the kitchen, a room with walls painted a yellow that was a few shades too bright for comfort. The modern appliances were all stainless steel, an appropriate match for the luxurious marble topping the counters and large center island. A row of four elaborate stools arranged on one side of the island invited cozy conversations while the cook worked. Aside from two cereal dishes and two cups in the sink, the room was neat.

A family room adjoined the kitchen, and while it was clearly lived in, it was also clean. The cushy leather furniture was arranged for viewing the huge flat screen TV. Beyond that, a large window offered a wonderful view of the woods surrounding the house. Molly bet they saw plenty of wildlife in their backyard.

Not long after Molly and Lindy arrived, there was a knock at the door. Molly was closest, so she hurried to greet the delivery driver from The Hamper.

"I've got tons of food." An energetic young woman with *Melissa* on her name tag indicated the van idling beside Molly's car. "They told me to check before I unloaded stuff because people might not be home yet. But here you are." She smiled as if Molly had done something great, then trotted to the van and threw open the back door.

By the time everything ordered was delivered, the kitchen counters were covered with trays of small sandwiches and wraps, veggies and dip, fruit and dip, and desserts. Two large bags of potato chips and one bag of tortilla chips with accompanying salsa completed the food order. Gallon jugs of iced tea and lemonade cooled in the refrigerator.

As Melissa drove away, Molly and Lindy explored the rest of the downstairs for the best place to serve the food. Opposite the kitchen was a dining room, which opened into a large living room. Both rooms were beautiful, like spreads in a home decor magazine. Here the walls had escaped the eye-searing yellow and were covered in shiplap paneling covered in a soft whitewash.

A wall of windows framed Loch Mallaig, a vast expanse of blue reflecting the sky above. A pair of motorboats sped across the water, while a sailboat went at a more measured pace, its colorful sails billowing in the wind.

"This is a wonderful house." Lindy stood enthralled by the view. "If I lived here, I would never leave this room."

Molly thought of the little dance studio Janae and Verna ran as she gauged the value of this house and its contents. *Blackmail must be a very lucrative sideline.*

"Let's put the food in the dining room." Molly started back toward the kitchen. "Then you can admire the view as long as you want."

Lindy turned from the window and surveyed the large living room. Doubt and uncertainty crept into her expression. "We can't give her anything as fancy as this place," she said quietly.

Molly stopped in her tracks. "You've got things that are far more precious than leather sectionals and vaulted ceilings. You've got love and genuine caring. You've got honesty instead of secrets. And you've got you. What more could Skye ever want?"

Lindy hugged Molly. "I hope she'll feel the same way."

It didn't take long to set out the buffet of goodies, which were already neatly arranged on trays. They decided to put the beverages on the sideboard that sat against the wall under a beautiful watercolor painting of the lake in autumn.

As Molly went back to the kitchen to find an ice bucket, the house phone rang. She stared at it hanging on the wall by the kitchen table. She hesitated to answer someone else's phone, but then she thought it might be Verna calling with more instructions.

She picked up the receiver on the fourth ring. "Hello? This is—" Molly didn't get out her name before she was interrupted.

"You think you're so clever, don't you?"

The hairs on the back of Molly's neck rose at the angry voice. It belonged to a woman. Was it Wanda Joy Kowalski?

"Well, you're not clever," the caller continued. "What you are is sick. And cruel. Feeding off the mistakes, the pain of others. No more, lady. No more!"

The phone went dead.

Molly was still staring at the receiver when Verna walked in the back door. "Skye's driving home with a couple of friends who came to the ceme—" She noticed Molly's expression and went on alert. "What's wrong?"

Molly shook her head and finally hung up the phone. "A nasty call."

"A woman with a gravelly voice ranting and raving?"

"She's called before?"

"Several times, though it started just recently," Verna said. "I listened to the first call in shock. Now I hang up as soon as she starts talking."

"Is it always the same person?"

"As far as I can tell, but I don't know who she is."

"Are the calls for you?" Molly figured they weren't, but she wanted to ask all the same.

"Me?" Verna appeared shocked at the very idea. "Who'd be mad at me? I haven't got an ounce of backbone. My headstone will say 'Here lies Verna, who backed down and gave in at every opportunity.'"

"Don't be so hard on yourself," Molly said. "Being a nice person isn't a bad thing."

Verna shrugged as if she didn't quite believe Molly. "So far Skye hasn't answered any of these calls, thank goodness. Her friends only call on her cell phone." Verna shuddered. "I don't want her to hear the spite and hate. I don't want her asking questions I don't want to answer. Janae might not have been the best mother, but she was the only one Skye had."

"You think it's one of Janae's victims?"

"What else could it be?"

"Someone needs to tell her Janae's dead. Whatever she did is still a secret and she's safe."

Verna nodded, then seemed to realize she'd agreed to something she shouldn't know anything about. She tried to act confused. "One of Janae's victims? What are you talking about?"

Molly studied Verna for a moment, then glanced at the leather furniture and the latest appliances. She recalled the quality of the furnishings in the other rooms. "Verna, I know I'm going to offend you, but I've got to ask: how do you and Janae afford this gorgeous place right on the lake?"

Relaxing visibly, Verna answered easily. "It's no mystery. My parents left the house to me. They built it back when no one had ever heard of Loch Mallaig."

"And the contents? Did they come with the place?"

Verna laughed at the idea. "When Mom and Dad had the place, it was used furniture and mismatched linens. We loved it here."

"Have they been gone long?" Molly asked.

"About twenty-five years."

"And you've lived here since then?"

"I've lived here about twenty years."

Just a little longer than Janae had lived in Loch Mallaig, Molly realized. "So how did you and Janae become housemates?"

Verna's gaze slid away from Molly. "Did the food come?"

The fact that Verna had avoided the question meant the answer was important, but Molly went along with the change of subject for the moment. "It's all set in the dining room except for the ice cubes. I came in here to find something to put them in."

Verna opened a cupboard and pulled out a metal ice bucket. She handed it to Molly. "Thanks for all you've done."

"You're welcome. I'm glad we could help." Molly filled the bucket with cubes from the refrigerator. "So were you and Janae friends before she moved in? Or were you wanting to rent a room to someone?"

Verna coughed and pointed to her throat. She pushed past Molly and grabbed a glass from the cupboard, then filled it and drank slowly.

Molly waited until she put the glass down. "The question's not going away, Verna. Tell me about you and Janae."

Verna sighed and gave up. "She needed a place, and I needed money for modernizing."

"That sounds like a good deal for both of you. But there's more, isn't there?"

Verna opened the freezer and checked the ice cube supply. She stood there, her back to Molly, cold air forming clouds around her.

After a silent few moments she slammed the door and spun to Molly. Her face had paled to the same shade as the whitewashed shiplap in the front room. "At least I got Skye."

Molly furrowed her brow. "What do you mean?"

"I became like her aunt. I got to raise the girl, to show her love. Someone had to."

"She seems like a good kid."

"She's a wonderful kid." Verna appeared close to weeping as she ran a hand over the marble counter. "And she gets my house."

Molly set the ice bucket down with a thud. "What?"

Verna nodded as tears spilled over. "She doesn't know it yet, but she does."

Molly cringed. "Because Janae took it from you?"

Verna wiped the backs of her hands across her wet cheeks. "She knew how to hurt me the most. I didn't care that much when she forced herself into Dancing on Air. Of course I wasn't happy, but I remember thinking at least it's not the house." She grabbed a paper towel and blotted her face. "And then it was the house."

"What did she hold over you?" It had to be a secret Verna couldn't bear to have revealed.

Verna didn't bother to deny the blackmail. "We went out one night after Leaping Lowlanders not too long after she moved here. I was so surprised. I'm not the type of person people ask out for the evening. I'm too quiet, too introverted, too guilt ridden if you must know. Most of the time people don't even see me, let alone ask me to go out."

Molly felt a rush of sympathy at Verna's sad self-critique. "What happened?" she asked gently.

"I'm afraid of people, afraid I'll let something slip." Verna chanced a glance at Molly. "But she was so persuasive when she asked. She made me feel special, like she had chosen me to be her first friend in her new town. Janae, the vivacious, brave widow with the adorable daughter."

"And after that you found out who Janae really was."

Verna spread her arms in disbelief. "I didn't guard my tongue. Slowly she weaseled it all out of me. Oh, not my crime. I still guarded that information. But I told her I was from Montana originally, a rancher's daughter. I said I had a sister that I never saw anymore, that I'd moved to Loch Mallaig as more than a summer visitor not long before she did. Clever Janae. She did her research and figured me out."

She looked so devastated Molly felt her heart contract.

She was sobbing as she told Molly her long-guarded secret, declaring it as if she was reading a headline. *"Rancher's Daughter Kills Sister in Joyride Crash, Found Guilty of Manslaughter, Sentenced to Three Years."*

Molly felt as if the breath had been knocked from her. "Oh Verna. I'm so sorry."

"Lorna was only seventeen. I was eighteen. We went to a party together. We shouldn't have stayed when it got rowdy, but she insisted, so we did. See? No backbone. I was older. I should have said no, but I didn't. On the way home, we laughed and laughed at all the funny things that happened at the party. I was going way too fast and goofing off. I looked at her as I told a story, and I missed a curve. She died instantly. It happened almost forty years ago, but I still have nightmares."

"Oh Verna," Molly repeated, not sure what else to say.

Verna sank onto one of the stools and clenched her hands in her lap. "Losing Lorna nearly killed my parents. They never recovered, though they never turned their backs on me. Their unfailing love made me feel worse, but I don't know what I would have done without it and them. They died before their time, from all the stress, so I killed them too."

Molly rested a hand on Verna's shoulder. "Don't worry. Your secret's safe with me. Have you ever thought it would lose its power if you let people who are important to you know?"

Verna shrugged. Emotionally spent, she hunched over. "I don't think I care about anything anymore except how Skye will see me if she finds out."

"Well, she won't learn it from me. You have my word."

The women were quiet for a few minutes, the only noise the ticking of the wall clock. At one point, Lindy walked to the kitchen but stopped when she saw Verna with her head bowed. Molly shook her head and Lindy faded quietly back to the living room.

"Janae said, 'Let's make a trade.'" Verna's voice was suddenly bitter. "She'd keep my secret if I'd make her my business partner. What choice did I have?"

Secrets, Molly thought. *Binding. Imprisoning. Strangling.*

"At first she just wanted to be equal partners," Verna continued. "Then sixty-forty, and guess who had the sixty? Then to live here." She swept a hand around. "Then to be part owner, then full owner. And I buckled every time." She put her head into her hands and her words became muffled, but still clear enough to understand. "I don't want people knowing I killed my sister. I couldn't bear the whispers, the condemnation."

The front doorbell rang, and Lindy's voice spilled down the hall. "Come on in. Verna and Skye aren't available yet, but it should only be a few minutes."

Verna's head shot up, panic etched in her face. Without a word, she fled upstairs before anyone saw her.

20

Molly sat in her bedroom chair, relieved to finally be home after all the emotion of Verna's post-funeral revelations. The distraught woman had never come back downstairs after running off, so Molly and Lindy had stayed to help Skye manage the open house. They were event planners after all.

Skye had disappeared into her room with her friends not long before the last adults left the house, so Molly and Lindy had piled the leftover food into the refrigerator and let themselves out when they figured there wouldn't be any more mourners coming to call.

Now Lindy was resting, and Angus lay in Molly's lap, enjoying her attention after all his time alone. Molly rested her head on the back of the chair, contemplating Janae Harbison's most recently revealed victim. She couldn't decide which was sadder, Verna's life of guilt and grief or Janae's life of blackmail and backstabbing.

A knock interrupted her thoughts.

Angus, who adored guests, jumped to the floor and hurried from the room. He was vibrating with excitement near the landing door, waiting for Molly to hurry up and open it already. When she did, she blinked in surprise. Skye Harbison stood on the other side.

"Skye." Molly opened the door wider. "Come in."

"They told me downstairs that I could come up here this way." The girl entered the apartment hesitantly. "Can I talk to you for a minute?"

"Of course." Molly glanced at Lindy's closed door. Should she wake her?

"Is your friend here?" Skye asked.

"She's taking a nap. I can get her—"

"No!" Skye held up a hand. "Please don't. I need to talk to just you."

"Sure. We can chat in the kitchen." Molly led the way and gestured for Skye to sit at the table. "Can I get you something to drink?"

Skye shook her head as she sank into a chair and clasped her hands in her lap.

Molly sat across from the girl. "I'm sorry about your mom, Skye."

"Thanks," Skye said. "Everybody is, or at least they're saying they are. I'm trying to be." Immediately she looked horrified. "I'm sorry. I shouldn't have said that. It sounds awful."

"Shock and grief make us say strange things sometimes."

Skye gazed down at her hands. "The trouble is that I don't feel much grief. What I feel is mainly relief." Her gaze shot to Molly. "Relief! How's that for a daughter to feel over her mother's death? What kind of a terrible person am I?"

Oh, you poor child! Molly wanted to wrap her arms around Skye and rock her until she felt soothed and loved, but she resisted for the moment.

Skye rubbed her forehead as if she had a headache. "I'm sorry. I didn't come here to dump all my conflicting emotions on you."

"I take it as a compliment that you felt comfortable coming here. You can say anything you want."

Skye fixed her attention on Angus, who was sniffing at her feet. She began petting him. "I just need someone I can talk to honestly. You don't really know me or my mom. You don't care that I didn't like her. I mean *really* didn't like her." Skye sighed. "I can't talk to Verna. I'd only upset her. She liked Mom. She didn't seem to realize that she was sly and sneaky and not very nice unless she needed to impress you or get something from you."

If the circumstances had been different, Molly might have laughed at how far off the mark Skye was about Verna's relationship with Janae.

"And my mom didn't like me." Tears filled Skye's eyes as she brought her gaze to Molly. "She never liked me. What kind of a mom doesn't like her kid?"

Molly didn't have any answer. "Oh, honey. I am so sorry you feel that way."

Skye issued a shuddering sigh. "One of her favorite ways to start a sentence was 'If it wasn't for you . . .' If it wasn't for me, she could have been a star dancer. If it wasn't for me, she could have made a lot of money. If it wasn't for me, she'd have married a rich man. If it wasn't for me, she could have been happy. She thought I ruined her life even though I tried so hard to be good."

Molly leaned closer to Skye. "I can tell you with certainty that you did not ruin your mother's life. She had done a fine job of that before you were even born."

Skye's beautiful eyes brimmed with both an overwhelming need for reassurance and intense curiosity. "I knew I was right coming here. You can tell me things."

"I'm not the one you need to talk to."

"Right now you are. Like I said, you can look at things objectively."

Molly smiled slightly. "I don't know about that."

They sat quietly for a moment. Angus had put his paws on Skye's knee, so she lifted him to her lap, where he settled happily.

Skye smiled as she ran her hands down his back. "I always wanted a dog. Mom said no." She petted Angus for a few moments, then glanced up with a startled expression. "I guess I can get one now, can't I?"

"I guess you can. What kind do you think you'd like?"

"I don't know. Maybe one of those big dogs who love everybody. Labradors?"

"They're sweethearts." And her aunt Lindy had one.

Skye continued gazing at Molly thoughtfully. "The other thing Mom always said was, 'You look just like him.'"

"Your father?"

Skye nodded. "Like it's a terrible thing."

"How terrible can it be? You're beautiful."

"You think so?" There was such hope in the question that Molly wanted to weep.

"I absolutely do," Molly answered firmly. "You have gorgeous hair. It's such a wonderful color. And your eyes are pretty and kind. I love your dimple."

"Did my father have hair like mine? Eyes like mine?"

"I never knew him, Skye."

The girl's face fell. "Oh. I thought . . ."

"But I've seen his picture," Molly said. "You do have his hair and eyes."

Skye's smile could have lit an entire city block.

"You need to talk to my friend Lindy. She can tell you about your father."

Skye shifted in her seat, her smile melting into uncertainty. "Mom got really angry when she came to Leaping Lowlanders."

"Lots of memories for both of them."

"Bad ones?"

Molly nodded.

"But of what?" Skye asked. "I know your friend is from Mom's old life, the one she never ever talks about. She slipped once and told me she used to live in Chicago, 'where life was fascinating.' If it was so fascinating, why didn't she go back rather than make a martyr of herself here and make me miserable in the process?"

Instead of answering the big question, Molly shifted focus slightly. "I used to live in Chicago."

"Did you know my mom?"

"No," Molly said. "I never met her until I moved here."

"I didn't think you did. Does your friend live in Chicago too? Is that where she and my mom knew each other?"

"My friend is from Chicago, and they did know each other there a long time ago."

"Tell me what you know." Skye leaned forward eagerly, and Angus squirmed a little before settling again.

Molly didn't know what to say. Skye was eighteen, an adult, but she was still so young. The things that Molly knew would be hard for her to hear—besides, Molly wasn't sure she had the right to tell them. Shouldn't that fall to Lindy?

"How . . ." Skye stopped, took a deep breath, and tried again. "How did your friend know my dad? My mom never mentioned him. She never even showed me his picture. 'I don't have one,' she'd say. Who doesn't have a picture of her dead husband?" She shut her eyes and scrunched up her face, and Molly decided now was not the time to mention that Nate and Janae—or Alana—had never been married. "I've wondered if he was really dead. Or if he even existed. Maybe she made him up. But he must have existed, right? After all, I'm here."

"Like I told you before," Molly said, "I never met your father, Skye, but I've heard a lot about him. He was a wonderful man."

"*Was* a wonderful man? So he is dead?"

"Yes," Molly answered quietly. "I'm sorry."

Skye bent over and rested her head against Angus. "I feel sadder about him being dead than I do about my mom, and I never even met him. How bad is that?"

"Don't beat yourself up. You feel what you feel. You don't have to sort it all out today."

They were silent for a while. Then Skye asked, "So your friend can tell me more about him?"

"I think she'd be happy to."

"What's her deal?" Skye suddenly seemed suspicious. "Is she nice?"

"My friend—her name's Lindy Raymond—is very nice. You'll like her. You'd like her husband and her two kids too."

"So it'll be okay if I talk to her?"

"I think Lindy would like that a lot."

"What would I like a lot?" Lindy asked as she walked into the room. Her cheeks were flushed from sleep, and she was running her hands through her hair to untangle it. Molly hadn't even heard the den door open.

Lindy saw Skye and stopped, frozen with surprise and delight.

Skye stood, her body language screaming uncertainty and hope. "Mrs. Ferris says you knew my father."

"Oh, my dear, I knew him well." Lindy flew across the room and wrapped her arms around the surprised girl.

Skye stared at Molly over Lindy's shoulder, her eyes wide with astonishment.

Molly tapped Lindy on her back. "You're scaring the girl, Lindy."

Lindy stepped back immediately. "So I am." She indicated the chair Skye had just vacated. "Sit and I'll tell you everything. But first I have to get something."

Lindy raced to her room and returned with her purse. She rummaged for a moment, then pulled out her small photo album. She leafed through until she found what she was looking for. She removed the photograph from its plastic sleeve and held it out to Skye. "Your father."

Skye took the picture and stared at it. She touched Nate's dimple, then her own cheek. She ran a finger over his hair, then toyed with a lock of her own.

"You look so much like him," Lindy said. "I knew who you were the minute I saw you."

"Why do you have his picture?" Skye asked.

"Oh my goodness, I haven't said, have I?" Lindy laughed. "Your father was my brother, sweetheart. I'm your aunt. We're family."

Skye, eyes full of uncertainty, looked to Molly.

"It's true," Molly confirmed.

Skye stared at Lindy, so surprised that she couldn't speak.

Lindy reached across the table and took Skye's hand. "Let me tell you all about him."

Molly rose and left the room. It was time for Skye and Lindy to get to know each other and for Lindy to answer her niece's questions. Molly would only be in the way.

She nearly skipped down the steps to the bakery, eager to share news of what was happening up in her apartment with Carol and Laura while she helped them with the end-of-day kitchen cleanup. The spring in her step faded about halfway down the staircase, however, when she was struck by a sickening realization.

Because of her arrest and conviction for her sister's death, Verna's fingerprints would have been on file in the national registry. She could have changed her name when she moved to Loch Mallaig all those years ago—from Wanda Joy Kowalski to Verna Donnelly. She'd also "found" Janae's body.

Earlier that day, had Molly been comforting Janae's killer?

21

Guid Nychburris Day couldn't have picked better weather. Cotton-ball clouds dotted the brilliant blue sky, and the lake sparkled with sun jewels dancing in the soft breeze.

Molly parked the Bread on Arrival delivery hearse as close to the festival booths as she could, then she, Bridget, and Lindy ferried the trays of pastries and beverages on foot the final distance.

"Keep an eye out for Skye," Lindy said as they walked. "She's going to help us until Mike and the kids get here."

"And you didn't know she existed until this week?" Bridget was fascinated by the story.

"Never even suspected," Lindy answered.

When Skye approached them hesitantly, Lindy, arms full of baked goods, smiled brightly. "Good morning."

Skye lifted a hand in greeting, her dancer's grace making the motion beautiful despite her clear trepidation. "Hi."

Molly handed Skye a tray. "Follow Bridget and your aunt. And thanks for coming to help."

Now that she had a purpose, Skye's tense shoulders relaxed, and she trailed the others to the booth.

Once they'd arranged everything and had started selling their goods, Molly tingled with satisfaction. The tent Fergus had loaned them gave the bakery's booth a substantial footprint, the sign showed that they were established, and the plaid blankets spread over the tables were just the touch of color she had planned, along with the wildflower bouquets Bridget had arranged.

Molly did a mental count of everything they'd set out and came up one short. "There's one more tray of scones still in the hearse," she told the others. "I'd better go get it."

Bridget, busy bagging an order of cinnamon scones, nodded. Lindy was taking money for shortbread and bottled water and didn't seem to hear. Skye glanced up from breaking open a package of napkins and smiled acknowledgment.

A teen girl that Molly recognized from the previous day's funeral approached the booth, and Skye proudly sold her some chocolate-dipped shortbread. When she finished with her sale, Skye pulled Lindy over. "Julie, this is my aunt Lindy. She's visiting from Chicago. She's my dad's sister." The pride in Skye's face made Molly's heart melt.

She was still smiling as she weaved through the wide variety of booths. Her end goal was the hearse, but she wanted to take a few minutes to scope out the other vendors in case they had bright ideas she could incorporate for the bakehouse's booth next year. She passed jewelry presentations, woodworking displays, and original art hanging on clotheslines, most of which embraced the festival's Scottish theme. An ATM machine sat conveniently between the craft sellers and the food booths. In an opening between a popcorn booth and a smoothie seller stood a magician, his hands working at an amazing speed as he kept his audience spellbound.

She passed The Knit Hoose's booth, manned by members of the Fair Knitting Ladies. They were selling beautiful handmade sweaters, blankets, and winter accessories, with all proceeds supporting the Loch Mallaig Volunteer Fire Company. Aileen Morrison, who owned The Knit Hoose and led the knitting club, had set up a treadle spinning wheel and was working a basket of wool into yarn. A gaggle of kids watched as she explained what she was doing.

Molly waved at Greer as she passed the Loch Mallaig Police Department booth, and she noticed it was all hands on deck. Officers would spend the day wandering conspicuously among the crowd with their eyes out for trouble—pickpockets loved crowds like this. She wondered fleetingly if the photo of Wanda Joy Kowalski had come through yet. Would it reveal that Janae's murderer was someone they all knew? Molly quickly pushed down her fear that it would prove Verna was the killer and decided to worry about it later.

A crowd of people were gathered around a TV at the next booth. As Molly got closer, she realized that they were watching the video Dallis had created.

"Was that really you?" A middle-aged lady pointed to the photographs of the old Dallis mounted on the back wall of the booth beside pictures of the buff Dallis running a marathon, kayaking in white water, hiking a mountain, and, of course, dancing the Highland fling in full Scottish garb.

"Really me," Dallis said with his signature gleaming smile.

"But you must just have good genes." She shook her head. "I'll never look like you."

"The important thing is being healthy and gaining confidence. If you work at it like I did, you can feel as good about yourself as I do." He held out a clipboard. "Give me your information, and I'll contact you about getting started."

He noticed Molly over the woman's head and winked. She gave him a thumbs-up and wondered what Janae would think of the way Dallis had turned her threat into a triumph.

Next she searched out the Castleglen booth. She was curious to see what Fergus's son had done for his first foray into Guid Nychburris Day. As it turned out, his fresh ideas involved more than just a raffle.

A line of eager putters of all ages were waiting their turns at an artificial putting green. Neil had also set up a video driving range where participants hit a ball into a net and a computer told them the distance their ball would have sailed. A free dinner for two at the King's Heid would be awarded to the longest drive at day's end.

"If I thought I had a chance, I'd give it a try," Molly told Neil once he'd finished chatting with another passerby and sent him on his way with a glossy brochure and a free Castleglen pen.

"It's worth a shot," Neil said gamely. "Dad says your slice is improving, at least."

Blushing slightly at the fact that Fergus had mentioned their golfing lessons, Molly demurred and waved goodbye.

A few more local business owners called out greetings as Molly passed the booths on the outskirts of the fair. Molly smiled and praised their displays, exchanging pleasantries about the weather and the wonderful turnout.

The sounds of the festival—neighbors laughing, music playing on the loudspeaker, children shrieking with joy as they played on the nearby playground—faded slightly as she crossed the last handful of yards to the hearse. For the moment, she was alone, and she took the peaceful moment to appreciate how much she loved Loch Mallaig and everyone in it.

Heart full, she opened the back door of the hearse. The interior had been filled with baked goods a short time ago. Now the one tray, heaped with cinnamon and blueberry scones, looked quite lonely in the vast interior.

She leaned in to withdraw the industrial size tray. When she gripped the sides, ready to lift it out, she became aware that she wasn't alone after all. She turned her head and gave a little jump.

Isabella MacDuff stood too close for comfort.

"Hi, Mrs. MacDuff." Molly inclined her head. "You're good at sneaking up on people." She gave a laugh, trying to make light of the fact that, quite frankly, the woman's talent creeped her out.

Mrs. MacDuff said nothing, but moved a step nearer.

Molly grasped the tray by the sides and lifted.

"Leave it."

"What?" Molly blinked. Mrs. MacDuff was now so close she was almost touching the tray.

Molly automatically stepped back, trying to regain her personal space.

Mrs. MacDuff made a growling noise deep in her throat. Molly could think of no other word to describe the strange sound. The woman took a step forward. Molly edged back again and came up against the open door of the hearse. Mrs. MacDuff advanced again, and the only thing that kept her from being nose to nose with Molly was the tray of scones between them.

"Put them back," Mrs. MacDuff said.

"I can't. I have to take them to our booth."

Mrs. MacDuff shook her head. Her pretty red hair, usually so carefully combed, stuck out from her head like orange cotton candy. Her silver eyes glared with an intensity that made the hair on Molly's arms rise.

"I told ya to put them back." Mrs. MacDuff's accent had slipped again. "I won't tell ya again."

Molly knew an order when she heard one, but she was not removing the single barrier between her and this disturbed woman. She shook her head. "Like I told you, they have to go to Bread on Arrival's Guid Nychburris Day booth."

How was it that people were all around them, but they might as well have been the only people in the park? No one was paying them any attention. Well, except for a man walking toward them. Molly didn't know him, but she decided he was about to become her new best friend if Isabella MacDuff continued her strange behavior.

Mrs. MacDuff pointed at Molly. "Y'all are evil women. You and yer friends." Her Southern accent had completely taken over now.

Molly felt her mouth fall open. "What?"

"Evil! You used my son against me." Her face was twisted with emotion, but it was her silver eyes that made Molly swallow. While they were usually expressionless, whether blue or silver, now they burned with intent.

Molly opened her mouth to call to the only person who seemed to be paying any attention to them when Mrs. MacDuff slid her hand into the pocket of her plaid slacks.

"I got a gun." The calm voice the woman used to make that declaration was scarier than a scream would have been.

Molly could barely draw a breath. "A gun?" Did she believe her? Could she afford not to?

Mrs. MacDuff's lips curved in a smile, but her eyes remained as cold and venomous as ever. "A gun."

"You don't want to use a gun." Molly tried to sound conversational even though she could barely push out the words. "There are children nearby."

Mrs. MacDuff issued a derisive snort. "The only child I care about is my Robby, and y'all used him against me. You've taken him from me!"

"I don't know what you're talking about."

Apparently that was the wrong thing to say, because Mrs. MacDuff pulled out her gun. She held it just above the tray, its barrel pointed straight at Molly.

Molly's pulse pounded and her mouth went dry. "Mrs. MacDuff, you don't want to do this."

"'Course I do. Y'all used my Robby to set the police on me."

"What? When did I do that?"

"Y'all made him climb the crag and find the bat."

"I didn't," Molly said, trying not to sound too argumentative. "He was already at the top when Angus and I found him."

"No!" The little weapon vibrated in Mrs. MacDuff's hand with the intensity of her cry. "Y'all made him!"

"Wanda Joy." The brown-haired man Molly had almost called for help stood only a few feet behind Mrs. MacDuff. His voice was normal in volume, yet urgent. "Don't, Wanda Joy."

Mrs. MacDuff went rigid.

A strained expression filled the man's face as he stared at her back. Behind him several paces stood Chief Thomson and Greer. Did they know Mrs. MacDuff had a gun? Could they see it from their angle?

"Don't you say anything!" Mrs. MacDuff hissed at Molly.

"Wanda Joy," the man called. "Turn around. Look at me."

"Go away, Benson," Mrs. MacDuff replied. "Leave me alone!"

"Not going to happen, Wanda Joy," he said. "Not until you're in jail."

Molly gazed into the silver eyes, now full of panic and all the more frightening for it. "You're Wanda Joy Kowalski?"

Mrs. MacDuff flinched. No wonder she was worried about Robby and the bat. Her fingerprints were on it.

"Think of Evan, Wanda Joy," Benson said.

Who's Evan? Molly was lost.

"Robby!" Wanda Joy spun, pointing her gun at Benson. "He's Robby!"

The man retreated a step, his arms held out protectively. Behind him, Chief Thomson and Greer pulled their weapons in response to Wanda Joy's. Passersby saw the action and began to scream and scatter.

Benson kept his eyes fixed on Wanda Joy. "Of course. Robby. How could I forget? Well, think of Robby, Wanda Joy."

Wanda Joy had apparently forgotten all about her anger at Molly, who took a deep breath now that the gun was no longer on her. Scanning faces, Molly noted Benson's obvious fear, then glimpsed Chief Thomson's determination and Greer's careful movements to flank Wanda Joy.

Without stopping to think, to let herself be afraid, Molly lunged forward, ramming the tray of scones into Wanda Joy's back as hard as she could. The scones jumped on impact and three tumbled to the ground.

Wanda Joy screamed as she stumbled from the force of Molly's attack, and she grabbed her back where Molly had hit her with both hands. Her gun fell to the ground.

Everyone—Benson, Chief Thomson, Greer, and Wanda Joy— scrambled to recover the weapon. Molly knew Wanda Joy was going to grab it first. The woman was closest and she was desperate.

Molly flipped her tray from flat to vertical. Scones rained down around her as she swung it sideways, whacking Wanda Joy and sending her sprawling to the ground. Then with one deft step forward, Molly kicked the weapon away.

Benson snatched it up, and for a moment Molly feared she might have stopped one lunatic only to offer opportunity to another. She staggered in relief when Benson handed Chief Thomson the gun.

"No!" Wanda Joy wailed as the police officers closed in. "Robby!"

"You stole him from me for eleven years, Wanda Joy." Benson, his expression hard and unyielding, stared at the weeping woman as Greer cuffed her. "Now he'll be mine for the rest of his life."

22

"Now he'll be mine for the rest of his life,'" Molly repeated for her audience later that evening in her apartment. The space was barely large enough to accommodate Lindy and her family, who were clustered around Skye. Verna stood a bit off to the side, hands clasped in front of herself.

What an amazing day it had been. Molly had been held at gunpoint and helped subdue a dangerous woman. The booth she'd labored over had successfully sold out of every last baked good they'd prepared—aside from the upended scones that had fallen off her tray-turned-defensive weapon, of course. After the excitement around Wanda Joy's arrest had abated, Molly and her friends had danced with The Leaping Lowlanders without missing a step, though Molly knew that most eyes had been on Skye, the undeniable star of the performance.

And she had the honor of witnessing the beautiful, poignant meeting between Skye and Lindy's family, the grandmother, uncle, and cousins the girl hadn't known existed until just the day before.

Now Molly was weary and wired, a strange combination.

"So she kidnapped him and his dad had no idea where he was?" Marin, Lindy's bright-eyed, fifteen-year-old daughter, asked. "That's pretty wild."

Lindy's husband, Mike, had driven Marin, her brother, Chase, and Lindy's mother, May, over from Chicago that day, and they had arrived in Loch Mallaig after lunch. They were all settled at the Two Scots

Guesthouse—quite a bit less dodgy than the Hiegate Hostelry that Rick Capuana and his bodyguards had checked out of without a trace.

Molly fixed a somber gaze on the teen. "It is wild, but now father and son will be reunited."

"Because the kid's mom is going to jail for kidnapping." Chase, Lindy's thirteen-year-old, was entranced by all the drama.

"And murder," Marin added.

"So," Lindy said, "Robby MacDuff was born Evan Kowalski."

"Right." Molly poured herself more coffee from a stainless steel carafe on the table, then held it up to offer for anyone else needing a refill.

Lindy held out her cup and nodded thanks when she topped it off. "And Isabella MacDuff is really Wanda Joy Kowalski."

"Right." Having no more takers, Molly set down the carafe. "She's Robby's—Evan's—mother, and Benson Kowalski is his dad. He's the guy who showed up today."

"Where's he been for the past eleven years?" Mike Raymond asked. He was clearly as fascinated by the soap opera his wife had stumbled into on her vacation as his children were.

"It's not where he's been." Molly herself was still amazed at the story. "It's where she's been. Benson is in the Army, and when he was deployed, Wanda Joy decided she didn't like being a military wife anymore and took off with Robby, who was two at the time and his father's pride and joy."

"That's when the feds got involved?" Chase asked, eyes wide. "After the kidnapping?"

"The feds?" Mike studied his son. "You are definitely watching too much TV."

Molly laughed at Chase's shrug. "You're right, Chase. Benson reported Evan kidnapped. Kidnapping a child is a federal crime, especially when it involves taking the child across state lines. She falsified their identities and brought him from Alabama to Michigan. People have been searching for Wanda Joy and Evan for years, but she hid them in plain sight with her whole MacDuff clan claim to fame story. No one suspected who she really was."

"Except Alana." Lindy put an arm around Skye's shoulder as if to protect her from hard truths about her mother.

"Except her," Molly confirmed. "Everybody thought Isabella MacDuff was a little strange, but Janae sensed there was more. We'll never know how she figured out the truth about Wanda Joy and Evan, but she did. I'd say she only learned it recently because things happened recently, but that's only a guess."

Skye leaned forward. "Do you think Mrs. MacDuff meant to hurt my mom when she met her that night?"

Molly considered it for a moment. "I don't think so. She didn't have her gun with her like she did today. She meant to threaten me today. I knew I was in trouble when her Southern accent got thick. I heard that once before, earlier this week. I thought she was only concerned then because Robby was at the crag about the time Janae was killed. Now I know it was because she was afraid he'd seen her kill Janae."

Lindy nodded. "I think that she just grabbed the bat that had been left there."

"I've been wondering where that bat came from." It was the first time Verna had spoken.

Molly and Lindy exchanged a glance, then silently agreed to leave Bitsy out of the conversation.

Molly shrugged. "Maybe the police will tell us sometime." There were some secrets worth keeping for a friend—especially a friend who had pulled Molly aside at the festival and shared that she was leaving the next morning for a treatment center near Ann Arbor.

"I'm worried about Robby." Skye's face showed her concern. "I know what it's like to have a difficult mom."

"I know what it's like to have a difficult mom too," Chase said as he reached for another cookie and Lindy brought her hand down on his to stop him.

"It's going to be hard for him, Skye." Molly had been concerned about the boy too. "He's only thirteen."

"What do you mean, *only*?" Chase asked, clearly offended.

"How'd you like to lose me or your mom?" Mike asked. "Or how'd you like to learn you really belong to someone you never met before or can't remember?"

"I knew it." Chase poked his father. "I'm adopted. I thought I was too cool to be related to anyone in this house."

Molly swallowed a grin. Life in the Raymond house must be interesting with Chase around. "Robby will have his dad to help him, but he's not only moving someplace new where he knows no one. He's also learning he's Evan Kowalski, plain kid, instead of Robert MacDuff, future clan chieftain."

"I just hope his dad's nice." Skye still seemed troubled.

Molly smiled at the girl. If they needed proof that she was a good kid, this concern for Robby showed everyone where her heart was.

Verna folded her arms with a scowl. "I bet Janae made an overture of friendship to Wanda Joy like she did to me. She was good at wheedling secrets out of you."

Molly nodded. "She'd find the one thing people were willing to go to great lengths to protect."

"That's how she got me," Verna said.

Skye rose and went to Verna. She knelt in front of her and took her hands. "But her bargains don't mean a thing now that she's gone. Not one thing. I told you, Verna. I won't take your house.

It's yours. Your parents gave it to you, not me."

Her face filled with love for the girl, Verna cupped Skye's cheek in her hand. "But you know it's your home, right? Always?"

"I do." Skye smiled. "You can't get rid of me that easily."

Lindy glanced at Mike, then at Verna. "Verna, you are now part of our family, just like Skye. She told us she's a package deal, and we think that's wonderful."

"Maybe they'd like to stay with us for a week at the lake?" Verna suggested timidly to Skye.

"That's a great idea." Skye beamed. "And I'm going to visit them in Chicago and work with Aunt Lindy this summer. Who knows? Maybe I'll become an event planner."

Lindy held up a finger. "But only after you graduate from college, young lady."

Skye stared at Lindy, seemingly uncertain how to react to the firm mandate.

Marin reached over and patted Skye on the back. "You'll get used to her, Skye. It might take a while, but you will. We did."

Lindy put the back of her hand to her forehead. "Thankless child."

"And wait until she won't give you your allowance unless you clean your room." Chase grinned at his mother. "Shameless abuse of power."

"And she learned it all from me, Skye." Grandma May grinned proudly. "She learned how to love from me too. Never fear you can do anything to lose our love. We always love our own, and you are one of our own."

Skye blinked back tears, clearly overwhelmed.

"Just think, Lindy." Mike smiled at his wife. "You came here to relax. You told me it's a small town where nothing ever happens."

Lindy laughed. "I guess I was wrong." She reached over and squeezed

Molly's hand. "I suppose I was wrong about something else. You do belong in Loch Mallaig, Molly Ferris. It's the perfect place for you."

"Apology accepted," Molly said with a wink.

A short while later, Molly and Angus walked their guests out, then stood at the fence until the taillights had disappeared. While Angus explored the yard, Molly gazed at the gorgeous evening sky, now awash in vibrant pinks and oranges.

As she breathed in the cool twilight air, she thought about Skye and Lindy's family, then about Evan Kowalski and his dad, and her heart filled to bursting with happiness that they'd all found each other. As she watched Angus trot from bush to bush, his tail wagging eagerly, her mind flashed back to Lindy's words.

You do belong in Loch Mallaig, Molly Ferris. It's the perfect place for you.

Molly grinned. Everyone was right where they were supposed to be, herself included.